Deacon Platt was twenty-two years old, and had been hearing about the Gunsmith for most of his life. He'd seen the gunslinger Ransom's move, but he had never seen the Gunsmith's. He'd never seen Wild Bill Hickok's move either, but everybody knew he had been the best. Some people said the Gunsmith was better.

Platt wanted to see Ransom and the Gunsmith meet face to face.

He wanted to see how legends lived . . . or died.

Don't miss any of the lusty, hard-riding action in the new Charter Western series, THE GUNSMITH:

And coming next month:

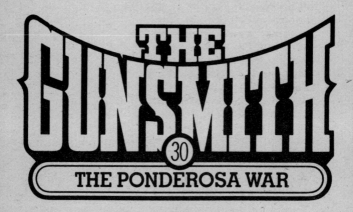

THE GUNSMITH

30

THE PONDEROSA WAR

J.R. ROBERTS

CHARTER BOOKS, NEW YORK

THE GUNSMITH #30: THE PONDEROSA WAR

A Charter Book/published by arrangement with the author

PRINTING HISTORY
Charter Original/July 1984

ISBN: 0-441-30903-8

Charter Books are published by The Berkley Publishing Group,
200 Madison Avenue, New York, N.Y. 10016.
PRINTED IN THE UNITED STATES OF AMERICA

ONE

The Gunsmith had sworn in the past that he would never return to the northern portion of the United States, since he and cold did not get along well, but after spending time in South America's heat and swamps,* the North didn't look so bad anymore. He would, however, avoid the Canadian border, which did not hold good memories for him at all.**

Upon entering the southwestern part of the Dakota Territory, the Gunsmith found himself slightly in awe of the trees. He had seen trees before, of course, but none to rival these. He swore that these were just shy of scraping the clouds—and then not by much.

The town of Olympia was located in a valley between two mountains, both of which were covered with these skyscraping trees. As he directed his rig into town, Clint Adams was still craning his neck to look up at them. He couldn't help wondering what it would be like to climb to the top of one, to be up that high.

Olympia was not a very large town, and Clint would

---

* *The Gunsmith #29: Wildcat Roundup*
** *The Gunsmith #12: The Canadian Payroll*

find out later that its growth depended heavily on the very trees he had been admiring.

After Clint had put up his rig, team and Duke—his big Arabian gelding—at the livery stable, he walked over to one of Olympia's two hotels with his saddlebags and rifle to get himself a room and a bath.

As he was signing in he looked at the clock behind the young desk clerk and asked, "Is that clock right?"

"Yes, sir," the clerk said without looking.

"I thought it was later than that," Clint said, frowning. He wasn't normally that far off in judging the time of day.

"That's okay," the clerk told him. "Happens to strangers in town all the time."

"What do you mean?"

"It's the trees," the clerk said. "They're so high up that they block the sun. It gets darker earlier in town because of it."

Clint grinned and said, "Really?"

The clerk nodded.

"You get used to it," he said, "when you've been in town a while."

"Well, I don't know how long I'm going to be in town," Clint said, "but I thank you for the information. Can I get a bath around here?"

"Through the back," the clerk said. "Can I get it ready for you?"

"Yes, please," Clint said. "I'll drop my gear in my room and come back down."

"It will be ready," the clerk promised.

Clint went upstairs and found that his room overlooked the street, which was completely in shadow now, even though it was barely past midday. He was becoming more and more impressed with the trees of the Dakotas.

He grabbed some clean clothes, and then went downstairs to wash off the trail dust, after which he was going to find a saloon and wash away the trail dust that covered his insides.

Olympia had two saloons, and Clint Adams simply entered the first one he came to. Feeling cleaner than he had in some time, he was looking forward to a cold beer and a few hours of poker, if he could scare up a game.

"What can I get you?" the bartender asked.

"A beer," Clint said. "A nice cold one."

"Only kind I serve, mister."

"Good."

When he brought the beer back the grizzled, nearly elderly bartender said, "Stranger in town, huh?"

"Yeah."

"Bet you can't guess what time it is."

"If I wasn't an honest man, I'd take you up on that," Clint said.

"Oh," the bartender said. "You heard, huh?"

"I heard."

The man shrugged and said, "Gotta make extra money any way you can, these days."

"Sure."

Clint turned his back to the bar to survey the room. There were about ten people all told, with five men seated at one table playing poker. There were three at one table, and two at another, just drinking. They were all good-sized men, too.

"They grow them big, hereabouts, don't they?"

Clint asked the bartender.

The old man, who was barely five two himself, said, "They all look big from where I sit, son, but yeah, they are kinda big around here. That's 'cause they're all loggers."

"Loggers?"

"Big strappin' fellas who cut down trees," the bartender said.

"They cut down the trees," Clint said. "God, but there are a lot of trees out there!"

"Not as many as there used to be, son," the bartender said, "and pretty soon there won't be as many as there are now, but you know what they call that, don't you?"

"Yeah," Clint said, "I think I do, friend. They call that progress."

"Yep, that's what they call it all right."

Cut down all those beautiful trees in the name of progress? Clint thought, shaking his head.

"Progress," he said again, but anyone within earshot would have thought he was uttering a dirty word.

Clint was about to order another beer when the batwing doors opened and in walked six men. Just as the men at the poker table were obviously loggers, the livelihood of the six men who had just entered was just as obvious, especially to the Gunsmith, who had seen a lifetime of their like.

They were gunmen, and things were just about to get very ugly in Olympia.

TWO

"Oh, shit," the bartender said beneath his breath. Obviously, he too had seen this kind before.

"You got anything under the bar?" Clint asked quietly, turning to put his empty mug on the bar.

"Scattergun," the man said, "but it's filled with birdshot."

"Keep it handy."

The way the six were aligned, it was evident who was the leader. Five of them were standing one step behind him, a tall, slender man with remarkably small hands who appeared to be in his early thirties.

"Any of you work for the Battles camp?" the leader asked aloud. All six men had pointedly ignored Clint and the bartender.

The question was answered in reverse, as the two men seated together rose and said, "Not us." Two of the men at the poker table likewise looked up and repeated the same words.

"The four of you get out," the man said, and all four men got up and hurried out of the saloon.

The remaining six men were apparently from the

Battles camp, and Clint noticed that they were all unarmed.

"You men work for Battles?" the leader asked.

"We got no beef with you," one of the men seated at the poker table said.

The leader of the gunmen said, "Who are you?"

"My name is Battles," the man said. "Tod Battles."

Clint noticed then that although Tod Battles was as large and beefy as the other men seated with him, he was somewhat younger. He scarcely looked old enough to be in a saloon, if you judged just from his facial features.

"You're Battles's kid brother, ain't you?" the man asked.

"I'm Tod Battles," the kid said, standing up. "You fellas want something?"

"What we want from you," the leader said, "is to leave the trees alone. What we want from these others is for them to leave town, while they can."

"Tod—" one of the men seated at the other table began, but Tod Battles waved him quiet with his powerful right arm.

"These men work for me and my brother," he said. "They'll stay as long as we pay them."

"Is this kid speaking for you men?" the gunmen leader asked.

No answer.

"Will you live or die on his word?"

"That sounds like a threat," Tod Battles said.

"I'm talking to them, kid," the man said, "not you. Can't they talk for themselves?"

"Tell him!" Battles snapped at the other men in the room.

One of the men at his own table stood up and told Battles, "I didn't sign on to dodge no bullets," and left.

One of the men at the other table stood up, said, "Sorry, Tod," and was also allowed to leave.

That left four.

"What about the rest of you?" the gunman asked.

The man who had been about to speak earlier said, "If you guys would like to put those guns down, we could discuss this like men."

The other three voiced their agreement with that and Tod Battles said to the leader of the gunmen, "What do you say to that?"

"I say if you was old enough to carry a gun, you wouldn't be in this mess," the other man said. "You all brought this on yourselves."

As the man turned his body partially to his left to speak to his men, Clint saw his right hand begin to move towards his gun. He was sure that the leader's move would trigger the other five, and then a slaughter would take place.

"I wouldn't do that!" Adams called out, stopping the man in mid-move.

As the leader turned his face towards Clint, the Gunsmith got his first head-on look at him. His face was startling, because it was amazingly smooth and devoid of facial hair. He doubted that the man would ever be able to grow a beard of any kind, and yet he still appeared to be in his early thirties. In addition, he had startling blue eyes, with unusually long eyelashes for a man. In fact, Clint could almost swear that the eyelashes weren't real.

"Were you talking to me?" the man asked in a deceptively soft tone.

"I was," Clint said. "You and your men seem to be spoiling for some kind of a fight."

"What business is that of yours?"

"Well, I just can't stand to see unarmed men shot down in cold blood, that's all," Clint said.

"And what do you think you can do about it?"

"Well, for one thing," the Gunsmith said, "I could kill you where you stand if I see your hand move any closer to your gun."

Inadvertently, the man threw a glance down at his right hand, then brought his eyes back level with Clint's.

"You think you can do that and get out of here alive?" he asked.

"Frankly, no," Clint said. "I'd say you and your boys are probably pretty fair gunhands, but I do know one thing."

"What's that?"

"You would not be around to see how many of your boys I take to the grave with me. That much I promise you."

They exchanged glances for a while, and then the man said, "What do you suggest, then?"

"I think you ought to let these fellas be on their way," Clint said. "What comes after that we can discuss when they're gone."

The man hooked his thumbs into the front of his gunbelt, and then said to his men, "Let them leave, boys."

The other five men spread apart, moving away from the batwing doors.

"Go ahead, Mr. Battles," Clint said. "Take your men out of here."

"But, mister—" Tod Battles started, but the Gunsmith didn't give him a chance to get any further.

"Go on. They're your men, so they're your responsibility," he said.

Battles frowned, then said to his men, "All right, let's get out of here."

As they moved cautiously towards the front door, the leader of the gunmen threw Battles a casual glance and said, "This ain't over, boy."

"You know it ain't," the kid shot back, and then walked out the door after his men.

"Well, now," the leader said, "that just leaves you an' us."

"Yes, it does," Clint said.

"Boys," he said to his men, "take out your guns and put them on a table."

"What?" one of the men asked, as they all looked puzzled by the order.

"You heard me," the man said. "Our friend here don't like to see unarmed men shot down, so you take off your guns, and then the five of you can give him a lesson in what it's like to poke his nose where it don't belong."

"I ain't about to take a beating," Clint warned him.

"We'll see," the man said. He moved to a table, pulled out a chair and sat down while his men deposited their iron on one table.

"All right, boys," he said, and they began to advance *en masse* on the Gunsmith.

"All I see," the man told Clint, "is five men walking unarmed towards the bar. You kill any of them, I think you're gonna have a real problem explaining why."

Clint frowned. He didn't have to kill them, but even wounding an unarmed man was not an easy thing to explain.

"Son," he heard the bartender say behind him, "I think you just bought yourself a peck of trouble."

THREE

"Shit," Clint said, drawing his gun. He was afraid that in order to avoid taking a beating he was going to have to shoot first and explain later. During that explanation, the fact that he was the Gunsmith was going to have to come out, and then he'd have to leave town.

But all that would come later.

As he drew his gun, suddenly the batwing doors opened and two large figures came lunging into the room. The five men advancing on him began to turn, but before they could both of the huge figures slammed into them, sending them flying.

Their leader's hand flashed towards his gun, but Clint was on him before he could reach it. His right fist connected with the man's jaw, driving him backwards and over the table.

When Clint turned to face the others, he was impressed by what he saw. The two men who had rushed into the room were not merely holding their own against the other five—they were winning. Bodies were flying every which way and as one came backpedaling Clint's way he slammed a punch into the man's unprotected kidney area. As the man dropped to

11

his knees, Clint turned to check on the leader of the five, and was surprised to find that he was gone.

"The back way?" he asked, turning to the bartender.

"Like his ass was on fire," the old man answered.

Clint turned and saw that the two men who had come to his rescue were rapidly cleaning house, so he said to the bartender, "Better set up three beers. My friends there are going to be thirsty."

As he watched the two men throw the last of his assailants through the batwing doors, he recognized one of them was Tod Battles. The kid must have taken his men outside, and then come back with help. The other man seemed to be an older version of the kid, maybe a brother?

"Gentlemen," Clint called out to them. "The beer is on me."

The two men exchanged glances, then marched to the bar and palmed their beers.

"I guess I owe you more than a beer," Clint said.

"Hell, mister," Tod Battles said, "you don't owe me, me and my men owe you. You sure pulled our fat out of the fire."

"Well, just maybe we're even," Clint said.

"Not by a long shot," the second man said. He extended a massive hand towards Clint and said, "I'm Tim Battles, mister, and me and my brother owe you a lot. I'd like to know your name."

"Clint Adams," Clint answered. "Are you two fellas brothers?"

"We are," Tim Battles said.

"This is Big Tim Battles, Mr. Adams," the bartender said. "He owns that mountain to the west of town."

"The mountain?" Clint asked. "The entire mountain? That sounds interesting."

"Well, actually it's more that we own the trees on the mountain," Battles explained. "It's a little bit of a long story, but it has something to do with what happened here."

"What do you mean?"

"Well, maybe me and my brother could buy you dinner on our mountain and explain it to you," Tim Battles said.

"Dinner on your mountain?"

"Sure," Tod Battles said. "We live on the mountain, we sleep on the mountain, we eat on the mountain—"

"And you come down here to get into trouble," Tim Battles finished for his younger brother.

"Tim—"

"Let's not argue about it here, Tod," Tim Battles said. "Why don't we take Clint up on the mountain and explain to him what he may have gotten himself into."

"Ahem!" the bartender said.

Tim Battles looked at the old man and said, "Damages, Cooper?"

"Damages," the old man said, surveying the wreckage in his saloon.

"Tim, why don't you take Clint on up the mountain. I'll be along when I settle damages with Cooper here."

"All right, Tim," said Tod, looking sheepish. Clint had the feeling that much of Tim Battles's time was spent paying for his brother Tod's damages.

Clint followed Tod outside while his brother settled up with the bartender.

After they had agreed on the assessment of the

damages and money had changed hands Cooper said to Big Tim Battles, "You may have gotten yourself a break you didn't expect today."

"Why do you say that?" Battles asked.

"Don't you know who that fella is?" Cooper asked.

"He says his name is Clint Adams," Battles said. "Ain't that who he is?"

"Oh, that's who he is, all right," Cooper said, "but that ain't *who* he is!"

"What are you talking about, Cooper?"

"His name is Clint Adams," Cooper said, "but they call him the Gunsmith."

"The Gunsmith," Battles repeated.

"You know who the Gunsmith is, don't you?"

"Yeah," Battles said, "yeah, Cooper, I know who the Gunsmith is. Thanks, Cooper, you just may be right."

"Don't thank me," Cooper said. "Just keep that kid brother of yours out of here. Everytime he comes to town something gets broken."

"Then why don't you refuse to serve him?"

"What kind of business would I have if I started refusing to serve people?" Cooper asked.

"Yeah, I guess you're right," Battles said. "Thanks for the information, Cooper."

"Sure, Tim, sure," the old bartender said. "I just hope you can make good use of it."

"Yeah," Battles said, walking out, "so do I."

When Clint Adams and Tod Battles mounted up and headed out of town, the man watching them from the shadows across the street had no trouble guessing where they were headed.

Battles Mountain.

The baby-faced leader of the gunmen who had just been routed from the saloon waited until Tim Battles left the saloon before leaving the protective shadows of the darkened doorway. Now he stepped out into the open and stared speculatively in their wake.

There was something familiar about the stranger, something that gnawed at the back of the gunman's mind. He knew him, he was sure of that . . . but from where?

When the gunman walked back into the saloon Cooper reached underneath the bar for his shotgun.

"You won't need that," the gunman said, "and besides, if you did pull it, I'd kill you."

Cooper touched the gun, then snatched his hand away as if it were hot.

"Good man," the gunman said.

"What do you want here, Ransom?" Cooper asked.

Bennett Ransom leaned his elbows on the bar and said, "I want to pick your brain."

"Meaning what?"

"You know who that stranger was, don't you?" Ransom asked.

"What makes you say that?"

"Because you know who I am, old-timer," Ransom said, "and I ain't never told you my name."

"I seen you once," Cooper said, warily.

"What did you see?" Ransom asked. For a man with such an innocent-looking face, Cooper thought, Bennett Ransom had the eyes of a dead man.

"I, uh, seen you kill a man once."

"Right," Ransom said, "then you must know that I enjoyed it. And I don't need much of a reason, either. So I'm only going to ask you this one time, Cooper,"

Ransom said, "only one time. Got that?"

Cooper nodded.

Ransom took his gun out and placed it on the bar top, just to bring his point home. He also enjoyed frightening Cooper. Maybe the old-timer would go for the shotgun after all . . . but not until he answered one question.

"Who was the stranger?"

"Clint Adams," Cooper answered immediately, staring at the gun on the bar. "They also call him—"

"I know what they call him," Ransom said, holstering his gun. Without another word he turned and left the saloon and Cooper let loose a sigh of relief.

Outside, Ransom was hurrying along to give a report to the man he worked for. He'd want to know that the Battleses had hired a gunman of their own.

They'd hired the Gunsmith.

FOUR

"We know the way, but we've still got to go slow in the dark," Tod Battles was explaining to Clint Adams as brother Tim caught up to them.

"You must know the way a little better," Clint commented to him.

"The horse knows the way," Tim said. "My brother just has to learn to trust the animal he's riding."

"I'm not much of a horseman," said Tod, "but I know enough to recognize a one in a million horse when I see one."

Clint noticed that Tim Battles was looking at him in a different way.

"Duke's special, all right," he replied, but he was still watching Tim, who was looking straight ahead now.

"Follow me," Tim said, suddenly urging his horse on ahead, "my horse knows the way."

Tod shrugged at Clint and said, "I'd rather walk, but by the time I got back dinner would be gone."

"It's still a little early for it to be this dark," Clint said. "The trees again?"

"You bet," Tod said. "Wait a couple of hours and then try and pick your way back to town in pitch blackness."

"I'm not looking forward to that," Clint said.

"Well, hell, maybe we can make room for you," Tod said.

"Would that be up to your brother?"

"Tim?" Tod said. "Don't take that 'Big Tim Battles' stuff too seriously. We're a democracy, here. The three of us share the load evenly."

"The three of you?"

"Me, Tim and Terry. You'll meet Terry when we reach the camp."

"I'm looking forward to it," Clint said. "Judging from the size of you two, I'm surprised the mountain is able to hold three brothers like you."

"Brothers," Tod said, as if he found that funny. "You're in for more of a surprise than you think."

"Great," Clint said.

He started to wonder what had happened to Tim Battles between the time they had left him in the saloon and the time he caught up to them, but it really didn't take much to guess. For every person who didn't recognize the Gunsmith by face or by name, there were two or three who did. That was thanks for the newspapers, and to his reputation.

Undoubtedly, someone had told Tim Battles who his new acquaintance was, and now it was playing on Big Tim's mind for one reason or another.

Clint was sure that he'd find out the reason once they got to the top of the mountain. All he could do was wait.

When he saw lights up ahead, he knew they had reached their destination.

"This is it," Tod said. "The top of Mount Battles."

"Is that what it's called?"

As they dismounted Tod said, "Not really, but I once read about a place called Mount Olympus—"

"And he's had delusions of grandeur ever since," his brother finished. "Let's get these horses taken care of and get into chow before it's all gone."

"Sure," Tod said, looking at his brother strangely.

"I'll help you, Tod," Clint said.

"Bring him inside when you're done," Tim said, and walked away.

"Something's on his mind," Tod said.

"Yes," Clint said, "and I think I might know what it is."

"What?"

Clint looked at Tod and said, "Where do we put up the horses?"

"We've got a makeshift livery rigged up," Tod said.

"Let's go there."

Clint followed Tod to a large tent rigged up with roped off stalls, and they unsaddled the horses, rubbed them down and made sure they were well fed.

"Now suppose you tell me what's on my brother's mind," Tod said, closing his massive right hand over Clint's right bicep.

"Jesus," Clint said, "relax that grip, will you, before you grind up my bones into dust?"

"Sorry," Tod said, letting go. "Don't know my own strength, sometimes."

"Christ, if you don't who does?" Clint said, rubbing his arm.

"What about my brother—"

"All right," Clint said. "I think someone in town

must have told him who I am.''

"What do you mean, who you are?'' Tod asked. "You said your name was Clint Adams.''

"It is," Clint said, "but some people put that together with another name, as well.''

"What name?''

Clint grimaced, and then said, " The Gunsmith," as if the two words soured his stomach.

"The Gunsmith!'' Tod said. "I know that name.''

"I was afraid you would,'' Clint said, "and your brother probably does too.''

"But that's great—''

"Why don't we go and talk to Tim and see if he thinks it's so great.''

"What makes you think he won't?''

"How old are you?''

"Nineteen, why?'' Tod answered. "What's that got to do with it?''

"People react to the same news in different ways, lad,'' Clint said. "Let's go talk to your brothers.''

"My brothers?''

"Yeah,'' Clint said. "Tim and Terry.''

"Oh, right,'' Tod said, straight-faced. "Let's go and talk to them.''

"Lead the way,'' Clint said. "I'm hungry.''

Tod led Clint to the center of the camp, where there were three wooden structures.

"Mess hall, bunkhouse and what?'' he asked.

"Bunkhouse?'' Tod repeated. "Yeah, I guess you could call it that. The other one, the small one, that's where me and my—where me, Tim and Terry live.''

"Uh-huh,'' Clint said.

"We also store equipment in the bunkhouse,'' Tod said.

"I smell food,'' Clint said.

"We've got a good cook, so you'll enjoy it," Tod said. "Tim ought to be inside."

"And Terry?"

"Terry . . . eats in the hut," Tod said.

Inside there were a couple of ten-foot-long wooden tables with benches on all sides.

"There are a couple of places over there by Tim," Tod said. "Grab a plate."

They each took a plate, utensils and a cup and walked over to the chow line, where their plates were piled high with meat and spuds, and the cups were filled with coffee.

Tod sat next to Tim, while Clint took the empty place across from the brothers.

"It's good," Clint said after tasting the food.

"I told you," Tod said. He looked over at his brother and said, "What's on your mind, Tim?"

"What?"

"Something's bothering you," Tod said.

"Not here," Tim replied.

"Clint thinks he knows what it is," Tod went on.

"He's probably right," Tim said, exchanging glances with Clint Adams, "which is all the more reason we shouldn't talk about it here. We can discuss it later, at the hut."

"With Terry too?" Clint asked.

"Yes," Tim said, raising his eyebrows, "with Terry too."

Clint and Tod exchanged glances and then devoted their full attentions to their food.

Tim Battles finished his dinner first and waited patiently while his brother and their guest finished theirs. When everyone was done he stood up and said, "Let's go and talk."

Clint and Tod once again exchanged glances, as if to

agree that neither one of them was a mindreader. They were just going to have to wait until the conditions suited Big Tim and he was ready to tell them exactly what was on his mind.

Tod Battles hurried ahead to walk beside his brother, and Clint followed the two of them to the hut where they lived. Tim opened the door and entered, but Tod stepped aside to allow Clint to go first.

"My brother forgets his manners when he gets like this," Tod explained, "and he gets like this when he's got something really serious on his mind."

"How often is that?" Clint asked.

Tod grinned and said, "All the time. You got to understand him to love him."

"I don't think I'll have to go that far," Clint said, and entered the hut.

Inside a fireplace warmed the room and joined with a kerosene lamp in lighting it. Tim Battles was sitting at a wooden table—a smaller version of the ones in the mess hall—and standing across from him was a woman.

"Clint," Tod said, with a grin on his face, "this is Terry."

It took Clint a few seconds to realize that Tod was talking about the woman.

"This is Terry," Tod went on. "Our sister."

FIVE

"Her real name's Teresa," Tod said, "but she likes Terry better."

Teresa Battles was a tall, solidly built woman in her mid-twenties with long, chestnut hair, tied back in a ponytail that reached past her waist. Her eyes were large, luminous brown orbs. She was big, like her brothers—though proportionately so—and although she had the strong Battles jaw, on her it looked good.

"Ain't you ever seen a woman before?" Terry Battles asked Clint.

"Oh, sure—" Clint stammered.

"The way you're staring at me, you sure couldn't tell," she said.

"He thought you were a man," Tod said.

"Is that so?" she asked, arching her eyebrows and thrusting out her impressive chest.

"That's not really fair—" Clint started to complain.

"I let him go on thinking you were another brother," Tod said, rushing to Clint's defense. "After all, the name Terry could just as well be—"

"Could we get to the point here?" Big Tim said.

"What is the point?" Terry Battles asked. "You've

got that look on your face, big brother—''

"Why don't we all sit down?" Tim said.

"Why don't I just leave," Clint suggested, "since I'm obviously the problem."

"Wait a minute," Tod started to protest, looking at his older brother.

"That's just it, Clint," Tim said. "I don't know if you're a problem or a blessing in disguise."

"How long do you think it will take you to decide?" Clint asked.

"What's going on here?" Terry asked.

"Terry, this is Clint Adams," Tim said.

And Tod added, "Otherwise known as the Gunsmith."

"Oh," she said, and then she stared at Clint and said, "Oh," in an entirely different tone of voice. Looking at Tim she added, "I think I see what you mean."

"Well, I don't," Tod said. "Clint kept me and some of the boys from getting our ears boxed. Why should having him around create a problem?"

"Because McCoy is not going to believe that this is just a coincidence," Tim explained.

"Who's McCoy?" Clint asked.

"He's going to think that we hired the Gunsmith to be on our side," Terry explained further to her younger brother.

"Who's McCoy?"

"So what?" Tod said. "Maybe that'll scare him."

"Or it might instigate something," Tim said.

"*Who is McCoy?*" Clint shouted, and all three Battles looked at him.

"Maybe we'd better explain," Tim said.

"We've got coffee, if anyone wants some," Terry said.

"Is it strong?" Clint asked.

She looked at him as if he were crazy and said, "Of course!"

"I'll have some," Clint said, and moved towards the table to sit down.

They all had a cup of coffee, and when they were all seated at the table—Clint and Terry side-by-side and close enough to bump shoulders—Tim Battles began his explanation.

Simply put, he said, when they had decided to buy this mountain and tame it—which is the way loggers referred to their job of cutting down the trees—they were not able to scrape together enough money. They'd been forced to finance the purchase through the bank of Olympia.

"Of which McCoy is the principal owner," Terry Battles added.

"This is starting to sound familiar," Clint said.

"I'm sure," Tim said. "We've got to get this timber cut and delivered down river, collect our money and pay off our loan—"

"—or McCoy steps in and takes over."

"Right," Terry said.

"And McCoy is trying to hedge his bet by hiring, uh, help, like those jokers in town," Clint said.

"So," Tod interrupted, "McCoy has hired gunmen, why can't we hire Clint?"

"Whoa, Tod," Clint said. "I haven't said that I'm for hire."

"And even if you were," Tim said, "how smart would we be to hire you?"

"What's McCoy got on his payroll?" Clint asked.

"A bunch of nothings," Tod said. "We showed him that in town earlier."

"What happened in town?" Terry asked.

Tim told her about the confrontation and then said, "Did you know the man you hit in the saloon, Clint?"

"No, I can't say that I did," Clint replied, thinking back, "although now that you mention it, there was something familiar about him."

"Would you know who he was if I said the name 'Ransom'?" Tim asked.

"Bennett Ransom?" Clint asked.

"Right."

"The baby-faced killer," Clint said.

"Right again," Tim said, "and by now I'm sure he knows who you are."

"Great," Clint said, shaking his head in total disgust, "that's all I need!"

"What's the matter?" Terry Battles asked. "Are you afraid of a man with a reputation?"

The look of disgust on the Gunsmith's face deepened at that remark, and for a fleeting moment Terry Battles felt ashamed of herself, and embarrassed.

Then she remembered who she was and tried to stare him down, like she did all men.

That was when she discovered that the Gunsmith was not like "all men."

SIX

"Say that again," McCoy said to Bennett Ransom.

"Say what again? About the Gunsmith?" Ransom asked, looking confused.

"Yes," McCoy said from behind his massive desk.

Bennett Ransom shrugged his thin shoulders and said, "Clint Adams, the Gunsmith, is in town and he's working for Big Tim Battles."

McCoy paused and cocked his head, as if he were listening to something only he could hear. He was a big man physically and—at least in the small community of Olympia—economically and politically too. He was in his early forties and sported a big, handlebar mustache that he was very proud of. He wore three-piece suits and fastidiously avoided any kind of dirt.

That included dirty work, which was of course why he employed Bennett Ransom, but he found that Ransom occasionally needed to be motivated.

Like now.

"What's the matter?" Ransom asked.

"I hear something in your voice that I don't like, Ransom," McCoy said.

"What?"

McCoy cocked his head that way again and listened a moment before answering. "I think—yes, I think I've got it now." McCoy smiled at Ransom.

"What?" Ransom demanded.

"Fear," McCoy said. "That's what I heard."

Ransom shook his head in disbelief.

"You're afraid of this man, the Gunsmith," McCoy said. "I can hear it in your voice."

It was a lie, of course, but it had the desired effect.

"I ain't afraid of anybody!" Ransom shouted, growing red in the face. If he had been sitting, he would have leaped to his feet, but McCoy was careful never to allow Ransom to sit in his office. It kept the man in his place—and it also kept the furniture in the room cleaner.

"You didn't kill him, did you?" McCoy asked, spreading his hands.

"I didn't know who he was," Ransom argued.

"So?" McCoy said. "You thought he was a nobody and you didn't kill him. Am I to believe that now that you know who he is you will become braver?"

"You told me not to kill anyone," Ransom said.

"I didn't know the Gunsmith was going to come into the picture, did I?" McCoy asked calmly.

"Well, neither did I."

McCoy shook his head as if he were dealing with a child who was incapable of understanding.

"Ransom, this is your business," McCoy said. "The man is in your business. You're telling me that you didn't know the legendary Gunsmith when you saw him?"

"I never came up against him before," Ransom argued.

"Well," McCoy said, joining his hands in front of

him, "you have that chance now, don't you? Don't disappoint me, eh, Ransom?"

"He's as good as dead, Mr. McCoy," Ransom said.

"Not until I say so, Ransom," McCoy said, sternly.

"But you just said—"

"I said don't disappoint me when I give the word," McCoy explained. "I haven't said the word yet, have I?"

"Mr. McCoy," Ransom said, hopelessly, "what do you want me to do?"

"What you're told, Ransom," McCoy answered, smiling slightly, "only what you're told."

SEVEN

After Terry Battles got up and stalked out of the room, Tim said to Clint, "I'm sorry about that."

"Forget it," Clint said.

Tod, who had stared after Terry until she disappeared out the door, said, "What was that all about? I've never seen her leave a room like that."

"Forget that," Tim said. "Maybe our sister finally learned herself a little lesson."

"What—?"

"We still have a problem," Tim said, cutting his younger brother off.

"You've got your problem," Clint pointed out, "and I've got mine."

"They're both the same, actually," Tim said to Clint, "when you think about it. Ransom's your problem, right?"

"I'm afraid so," Clint said. "If he really knows who I am, I'll have a hard time getting out of town without facing him."

"You mean, he'd want to try you out?" Tod asked, looking excited at the prospect of witnessing a gunfight.

"Well, he's working for McCoy, and McCoy is our problem," Tim said. "That makes them one and the same."

"Your logic is faulty," Clint said, "but I won't argue the point with you."

"All right, then let's get back to my original problem," Tim said.

"What?" Tod asked.

"Even if we don't hire Clint," Tim said to his brother, "McCoy will never believe we didn't. He'll never believe that the presence of the Gunsmith here in Olympia is just a coincidence."

"So?" Tod asked. "We went through this already. I still think that since Clint is here, we should hire him and his gun."

"My gun is not for hire, Tod," Clint said. The coldness in his voice made Tod Battles feel a chill.

"I'm sorry," Tod said. "I just thought—I mean, since you have the reputation—"

"Tod, why don't you go and find out where Terry went?" Big Tim suggested.

Tod, looking and feeling very embarrassed, nodded, stood up and left.

"He's young, Clint," Tim said, "and my sister —well, Terry is just Terry."

"I can't really blame them," Clint said.

"Look, I was worried about keeping you around, but now I see that it really doesn't make a difference," Tim said. "Stay up here with us."

"I might be better off just going back to town and leaving in the morning," Clint said.

"Do you think Ransom will let you do that?" Tim asked. "I mean, even if you manage to avoid him, McCoy is bound to send some of his boys after you.

What happens if that happens, and then you leave?''

"I can't afford that, either," Clint said. "If word got out that I was scared out of a town, I'll look like an easy mark for some would-be young gunslinger."

"I can see where having a reputation isn't the easiest thing in the world," Tim said.

"It takes time to learn how to live with it," the Gunsmith said, "and I've spent a lot of time trying." He looked down at the remnants of his coffee at the bottom of his cup and added, "Maybe one of these days I'll get it right."

He got up and walked over to the coffeepot to pour himself a second cup. He held the pot out to Tim, who nodded and extended his cup. Clint filled it, replaced the coffeepot on the hearth, and sat back down.

"We've got room," Tim said, "either here, or in the bunkhouse with the men."

Clint looked around the small hut and asked, "How do you think Terry would feel about my sleeping in here?"

Tim grinned and said, "Then you'll stay?"

Clint nodded and said, "I'll stay—the night, anyway. I can't say what I'll do beyond that."

"Good enough," Tim said. "I never meant to make you feel unwelcome," he added, extending his hand.

Clint took it and said, "Tod told me that I'd have to understand you to love you."

"And?"

Clint took the hand and said, "I told him I didn't think I'd have to go that far. Do you mind?"

"I don't mind at all."

Tim showed Clint where he could sleep and Clint commented on the seemingly unused beds in the bunkhouse.

"Well, McCoy's boys, especially Bennett Ransom, have succeeded in scaring off a few of our men," Tim confessed.

"Quite a few, from the looks of things," Clint said. "Actually, I saw a few leave earlier today."

"Yeah, and they didn't even bother coming back for their gear," Tim said.

"Has anyone been killed yet?" Clint asked.

Tim seemed surprised and dismayed by the question. Frowning, he said, "Nobody's even been hurt, it's been all threats so far. Clint, does someone have to get killed?"

"With Bennett Ransom here," Clint said, "I don't really know how it can be avoided. In fact," he added, "I'm surprised it hasn't happened already."

"Why?"

"With a man like Bennett Ransom?" Clint said. "His gun is the only way he knows how to solve his problems."

"Aren't you judging him pretty much the same way Tod and Terry judged you?" Tim asked. "By reputation?"

"It's not the same," Clint said.

"Why not?"

"My reputation was all Tod and Terry knew," Clint said. "I've got more than that on which to judge Bennett Ransom."

"You know him?"

"I know of him."

"That's the same—"

"My source is good, Tim," Clint interrupted, "and reliable. Ransom's a killer. If he's held back this long, it's because your Mr. McCoy is holding him back. What about McCoy? What kind of man is he?"

"Self-important, pushy, overbearing, likes to let

other people do his dirty work for him while he stays in his office, where it's nice and clean.''

"How powerful is he?''

"He's more like a big fish in a little pond,'' Tim said, "but I think he might be looking to use this mountain to grow a little. Why are you asking?''

"No reason, really,'' Clint said. "Just curious.''

"I see,'' Tim said. "See you in the morning.''

"You mind if I walk around your mountain a bit before I turn in?''

"Sure,'' Tim said, "just don't get lost, huh?''

EIGHT

Clint was walking in the dark, among the massive trees and the fresh air, when he heard someone behind him. He turned and found himself facing Terry Battles.

"Hello," he said.

"Hi," she replied.

She was a big, fine-looking woman who dressed like a man and, probably, tried to act like one most of the time, but at the moment she seemed almost girlish in her embarrassment.

"I'm going to do something I don't think I've ever done before," she said.

"What?" Clint asked, warily.

"Apologize."

"There's no need—"

"Yes, there is," she said, holding up her hand. "Tim told me what you did for Tod. We're very grateful."

"Did he tell you that they came back and saved my bacon as well?"

She shook her head.

"It's not the same thing," she said. "My brothers and I—well, I just want you to know that we don't

35

consider the score even, and for that reason I'm sorry about what I said.''

"Apology accepted," he said.

She nodded, then tried to cover the awkward silence that followed by saying, "Well, that wasn't as hard as I thought it would be."

"Few things are," he said.

They stood facing each other for a few moments, and then she said, "Well, I best be getting back," and started to back up a few steps.

"Terry."

"Yeah?"

"Uh, if you could wait a few minutes, until I breathe a little more of this fresh air, I could use a guide back."

"Oh," she said, "sure, of course."

"Thanks."

Clint looked up at the clear, starless sky and said, "How do you cut these trees down, anyway? I mean, they reach to the sky."

"Sometimes we start with the top," she said.

"The top?" he asked, incredulous. "How the hell do you start at the top?"

"We've got men who do that for a living," she said. "We call them high-climbers, and that's their job. To climb to the top and take off the upper portion of the tree. If you hang around here long enough, you'll find out that everyone has a particular job. We have peelers, buckers, choker setters, flume herders, river pigs—"

"River *what*?"

Terry laughed and said, "We have bolt punchers, skid greasers, fallers—"

"Fallers?" he said. "Now, wait a minute. You mean you pay somebody to *fall*—"

Terry laughed again, this time without reservation. Her face became almost beautiful. If it weren't for that strong Battles jaw . . . Still, her mouth was almost full enough and wide enough to carry it.

"No, that's not what it means," she said. "Why don't you stay around awhile and find out what all those terms mean?"

"It sounds like I'd have to stay a long time to do that," he said.

"Not very long," she said.

"No?"

"No," she said, shaking her head.

He studied her for a few moments, then said, "If you'll take me back to the camp now, I'll sleep on it."

"All right," she said.

He followed her back, studying her from behind all the way.

"Where is Adams now?" McCoy asked Bennett Ransom.

"He went up on the mountain with the Battleses," Ransom answered.

"All three?"

"Big Tim and the kid, yeah," Ransom said. "The girl was already up there, I guess."

"Do you have anyone watching to see if he comes back down?" McCoy asked.

Ransom's silence made the answer to that question obvious. *Oh, well,* McCoy thought, he really didn't hire Ransom for his ability to think and make decisions.

"All right, Ransom," he said, speaking very precisely, "have a man check Adams's hotel and see if he came back. If not, have a man keep an eye out. I want to know if Clint Adams spends the night on that mountain.''

"Yes, sir,'' Ransom said. "And then what?''

"And then I'll let you know what, Ransom,'' McCoy said. "Go ahead.''

"Yes, sir.''

As Ransom left an idea was forming in McCoy's head. Maybe having the Gunsmith around wouldn't be such a bad idea, after all . . . depending, of course, on what side he was on.

NINE

The following morning at breakfast Clint told his hosts that he had decided to go back to the hotel.

"Does that mean you're leaving town?" Terry Battles asked.

"No," Clint said. "I'll stay around awhile, but I think it would be smarter for me to stay in the hotel so it doesn't look like I'm choosing up sides."

"You're going to have to make a choice sooner or later," Tim Battles predicted.

"Possibly," Clint said, but he didn't discuss it further.

"What are your plans, then?" Tod asked.

"Well, to tell you the truth," he said, looking at Terry, "my curiosity was somewhat aroused last night about how you people do what you do up here. I'd like to learn something about it, if nobody minds."

The two brothers exchanged glances with each other, and then with their sister, and finally Tim Battles said, "Hell, we don't mind, but I'd say you better be prepared for a visit from Bennett Ransom."

"Or McCoy himself," Terry said.

"Why McCoy?" Tod asked.

39

"She's right," Big Tim said. "McCoy might try to hire you himself, Clint."

"If he does, he won't have any luck," Clint assured them.

"Why not?" Terry asked. "He can sure offer you more money than we could."

"Nobody could offer me enough money to work with Bennett Ransom."

"How about to replace him?" Tim asked.

"It doesn't matter," Clint said, "because I'd tell him the same thing I told you. My gun is not for sale."

After breakfast Tod asked Clint if he wanted to look around the camp right away.

"I think I'll go back into town first," Clint answered. "I'll come back up a little later, or maybe tomorrow morning, and then I'd be very interested in looking around and finding out just what river pigs and fallers really do."

"You're welcome anytime, Clint," Tim Battles reminded him. "Just do me a favor and keep an eye on your back while you're in Olympia."

"Tim," Clint said, "that's one thing I've sort of made a lifetime hobby of mine."

Tim Battles nodded, understanding. "Let's go, Tod," he said. "We've got some trees to knock down."

"See you later, Clint," Tod said.

As Tim and Tod walked away, Terry sidled up next to Clint and said, "Tod is fascinated by you."

"By my reputation, you mean," Clint said. "He's fascinated by the man he thinks I am."

"Will you be around long enough to show him what kind of man you really are?" she asked.

"Well," Clint said, turning as Duke was walked

over to him by a young logger, "I hope I've already shown him that."

"Of course," Terry said, embarrassed again. She was amazed at how this man was able to do that to her. Normally, she was able to handle men any way she wanted to. What made this one different? she wondered. "I'm sorry," she said.

"Don't keep apologizing," he told her, accepting Duke's reins and patting the huge horse's neck. "It's a bad habit to get into."

"Will you be back later?"

"Either later or tomorrow morning," he said. "Would you be the one to show me around? I mean, I wouldn't want to take your brothers away from their work—"

"—but I don't have any work to do, right?" she asked. "Because I'm a woman in a logging camp?"

He mounted up and then frowned down at the handsome, well-built young woman.

"Well, now *I've* said the wrong thing," he said. "It's my turn to apologize."

"That's all right," she assured him, "just don't keep doing it."

"What—saying the wrong thing or apologizing?"

"Either one would be a bad habit to get into," she told him.

"I'll remember," he promised. "See you soon."

As the man turned his big black horse around and started down the mountain, she found herself thinking, *The sooner the better*, and then became annoyed at herself for doing so.

Deacon Platt saw the man on the big black horse come riding down off the mountain and into town and brought the chair he was sitting in down onto all four of its legs with a bang, startling himself.

Hastily, he stood up and backed into a doorway from where he continued to watch the man as he rode down Main Street.

Ransom had told Platt who the man was, and Platt took advantage of his opportunity to get a relatively close-up look at a living legend.

"The Gunsmith, by damn," he said, beneath his breath. Platt was twenty-two years old, and had been hearing about the Gunsmith for most of his life. "I wonder," he said to himself, "if Ransom can really take him, like he says he can."

He'd seen Ransom's move, but he had never seen the Gunsmith's. He'd never seen Wild Bill Hickok's move either, but everybody knew he was the best.

Some people, though, said that the Gunsmith was at least as good as Hickok.

Some people said he was better.

Platt watched the Gunsmith ride into the livery stable, then come out a few minutes later and walk into the hotel. He waited a few moments himself, then went into the hotel lobby. He breathed a sigh of relief to see that Clint Adams was not there, and stayed only long enough to determine that the Gunsmith had not checked out of the hotel.

Then he hightailed it out of there to report his findings to Bennett Ransom. He didn't know how Ransom would react, but he was glad that the Gunsmith wasn't leaving town.

He wanted to see Ransom face him. He wanted to see the Gunsmith in action.

He wanted to see how a legend lived . . . or died.

TEN

Clint wasn't in his room very long when there was a knock at his door. He wasn't quite sure what—or whom—to expect, but was surprised by what he did find.

She was blonde and tall—though not quite as tall as Terry Battles—and the low-cut dress she was wearing made her obvious attributes even more obvious.

"Well, hello," she said, sauntering past him into the room.

He swung the door shut and said, "Hello, yourself. Can I help you?"

She turned to look at him, then smiled, reached behind her so that her full breasts thrust forward, undid the catch behind her dress and let it fall to the floor.

"No," she said, "but you can help yourself."

It took her only a second to remove her undergarments, and then she was standing there nude and inviting. Clint could feel himself responding to her large, firm, cherry-nippled breasts and the fine blond tangle of hair between her legs, but there was still that nagging question in the back of his mind that he always asked when things came too easy. And this was definitely too easy.

Why?

"Why?" he asked, voicing the one word that stood out in his mind.

She stared at him, hands on her hips, and said, "Well, you're certainly good for a girl's ego, I'll tell you that."

"Don't get me wrong, now," he said.

"Oh, I've got you wrong?" she asked, smiling. "Suppose you set me right, then." Then she frowned at Clint, looking concerned, "You don't prefer boys, do you?"

Clint closed his eyes and shuddered, thinking fleetingly of all the beautiful women he would have missed if . . .

"No," he said, forcefully, "no. There's nothing I'd like better than to climb into bed with you right now—"

"Fine," she said, moving towards the bed. Her breasts swayed invitingly as she turned down the blanket, slapping together lightly as she moved.

"But I'd still like to know why," he finished.

"You the kind of fella looks a gift horse in the mouth?" she asked, straightening up. He saw that her thighs were a little meaty, but he actually liked women with some extra meat on them. They made you know that you were in bed with *somebody*.

"Every time," he said.

"Well then, that's what I am."

"A gift horse?"

"No, silly," she said. "A gift."

"A gift," he said. "You mean that, under normal circumstances, I would have to pay for this?"

She frowned again and said, "Would you find that so offensive?"

"Definitely," he said.

"You're a strange man," she said, shaking her head.

"I just don't believe in paying for my pleasures," he said.

"That's just so much bullshit," she said, shocking him.

"What?"

"Do you like a beer," she asked, "or a drink after a long ride? Do you like a good meal?"

"Yes, but—"

"Don't you pay for them?" she demanded.

"Yes, but—"

"You're gonna tell me that's different, right?"

The situation had become ludicrous. Here he was defending his opinion to a naked whore he hadn't even invited into his room.

"Let's forget that for now," he said.

"Fine," she agreed. "We'll discuss it after."

"After what?"

She smiled and looked at the bed.

"Oh, wait a minute—"

"I got news for you, mister," she said, walking up to him now, bringing what appeared to be acres of creamy flesh within inches of him. When she got real close to him she put her hand on the bulge in the front of his pants and continued, "I'm too damned curious to leave this room without taking you to bed." She squeezed him and said, "Besides, I don't really think you want me to leave, anyway."

"What's your name?" he asked her.

"Candace."

"Candace, I never said I wanted you to leave," he reminded her. "What I said was 'why?' and I'll amend that question now. If you're a gift, I want to know who from."

"And then will you take me to bed?" she asked, rubbing the bulge of his penis through his pants.

Damn, he thought, things had gone too far for him not to, no matter who sent her.

"Yes."

She smiled, rubbed her turgid nipples against his chest and said, "McCoy."

ELEVEN

Clint pushed her towards the bed by palming both of her breasts and then shoving her back. She rested on her elbows while she watched him undress, and then settled down on her back as he joined her on the bed.

He kissed her hard, opening his mouth to accept her probing, insistent tongue, and laid his right hand over her pubic mound. While she continued to probe with her tongue, he did some probing of his own with his middle finger, dipping it into her. She dug her behind into the mattress as he wiggled his finger around inside of her, and moaned into his mouth.

When he released her mouth to run his tongue over her breasts she moaned again and then said, "Oh, mister . . ."

"Clint," he said. "When this is all over, we'll know each other well enough for you to call me Clint."

"Promise?" she asked, giggling.

He bit her nipple and wiggled his finger around for his answer, and her breath caught in her throat.

He sucked and bit her nipples until they were incredibly hard, then ran his tongue down the valley between her breasts, over her sternum to her belly, where he tongued her navel, and then farther still, until his tongue replaced his middle finger in the wet, steaming depths of her. He lapped at the sweet juices avidly, then found her stiffened love button and began to suck on it.

"Oh, Jesus . . ." she said, lifting her butt completely off the bed.

He continued to manipulate her with his tongue, and when he inserted a finger back inside of her at the same time, her body was wracked by pleasure waves. He had to use his elbows to pin her thighs to the bed as she seemed to be fighting to get away from him, although he knew that wasn't the case at all.

"Oh, Christ . . ." she moaned, and he knew that she'd had an actual orgasm, and not a "whore's orgasm."

"Give it to me now," she said, reaching for him.

He considered holding back from her what she wanted until she answered a few more questions, but the truth of the matter was that he wanted it badly, as well, and could not wait.

He moved up so that the bulbous head of his cock was probing the slick lips of her cunt, and then she grabbed him by the buttocks and forced him into her.

"Yes," she said, eagerly lifting her hips and grinding her pale hairs against his black ones, "oh yes, damn it!"

Suddenly she was all frenzied motion beneath him, and he was caught up in the pace. Her hot, cavernous pussy was sucking at him, as if furiously trying to force his orgasm from him.

He gritted his teeth as he drove into her again and again, and when she said, "Oh, sweet damn!" he relaxed all efforts at self-control and allowed a torrent of semen to explode inside of her. Hungrily, her insides continued to suck his seed from him as her nails dug into his buttocks, until there was nothing left for him to give.

"Oh," she said a few minutes later, "I forgot to tell you something I was supposed to tell you before we went to bed."

"What was that?"

"You won't tell, will you?" she asked. "I mean, that I forgot to tell you before . . ."

"I won't tell," he promised.

"Mr. McCoy said that I was supposed to tell you to go and see him after . . . we finished, and that he would consider your . . . acceptance of his gift as your assurance that you would."

Clint smiled, ran his hand along the inside of her meaty right thigh until it was resting on her pubic mound, and said, "That's his problem."

TWELVE

Actually, Clint did go and see McCoy, but not out of any feeling of gratitude or obligation. He simply wanted to meet the man, and hear what his offer would be.

It was bound to be a good one, because it had had a very good start.

McCoy's office, Candace said, was at the Bank of Olympia, and that's where Clint presented himself after he and the girl left his hotel.

"You can usually find me over at the Olympia saloon," she said, then added, "that is, if you ever want to find me."

"Well, I probably won't be returning to Olympia's other saloon. . . . Who owns the Olympia saloon?" he asked, just on a hunch.

"You obviously know the answer to that one already," Candace said. "The same man who owns the Olympia Hotel and the Bank of Olympia."

"I'll see you later, Candace."

"Ooh, I hope that's a promise," she said, and sauntered off to go back to work.

Clint walked over to the bank.

"I'd like to see Mr. McCoy," he told a thin, bespec-tacled man sitting behind a desk.

"Who shall I say wants to see him?" the man asked.

"Me."

The man waited for more, but when he saw that it wasn't forthcoming he said nervously, "Uh, yes, but who shall I, uh, say—"

"Tell him it's the man who always looks a gift horse in the mouth."

The man frowned, but decided not to ask any more questions. He was paid to run the bank, not question Mr. McCoy's "other" employees—and this man cer-tainly looked like one of the "other" employees, like Ransom.

"Just a moment," the man with the wire-rimmed glasses said, "I'll see if he's in."

"You do that."

Clint watched the man walk to the back of the room, knock on a door and enter. It was just a few minutes before the door opened again and spit the man back out.

"Mr. McCoy will see you," he told Clint. "If you'll follow me—"

"I know the way," Clint said, brushing past the man.

"Hey—" the man said, but that was the extent of his effort to stop the Gunsmith. And had the man known Clint's identity, he would not have even gone that far.

Clint entered the room without bothering to knock on the door. If McCoy was the kind of man he thought he was, the move should have thrown him off balance.

"McCoy," Clint said to the man behind the desk.

The man looked up and frowned from behind his almost comically huge handlebar mustache.

"People don't usually enter my office without knocking, Mr. Adams."

"Mark me down as the exception to that rule, McCoy," Clint said.

McCoy seemed about to come back with a sharp retort, but then bit it back. He cocked his head to one side as if he were listening to something Clint couldn't hear, and then his face seemed to relax.

"Mr. Adams, I think our relationship is getting off on the wrong foot," he said.

"What relationship, McCoy?"

"The one I hope we will have, after you've heard my offer—my very generous offer—of employment."

"Employment?" Clint repeated. "What about your man, Bennett Ransom?"

"Ransom?" McCoy said. "Ransom will be no problem at all. If you and I come to terms, he can be . . . dealt with."

"By whom?"

"By you, if you like," McCoy said.

"You mean you would want me to kill Ransom?" Clint asked.

"Why don't you let me tell you what my offer is, and then we can discuss the finer details later," McCoy suggested.

"I don't think so."

McCoy frowned, but said, "All right, then, we'll discuss the details—"

"No. I meant I don't think I'll be listening to your offer," Clint said.

"Why not?"

"I don't think I'd enjoy working for a man like you."

"A man like me?" McCoy asked. "Adams, I think perhaps you're prejudging me much too harshly."

"I don't think so," Clint said. "Any man who would employ a man like Bennett Ransom is nobody that I want to work for."

"That's ridiculous," McCoy said. "I'm prepared to offer you a lot of money."

"Do you know anything about me, McCoy?" Clint asked. "Anything at all?"

McCoy looked confused for a moment, and then he said, "Well, I know you by reputation."

"As what?"

Frowning, McCoy said, "As a gunman . . . a gun for hire, if you prefer."

"I don't prefer," Clint said. "My gun is not for sale, and it is not for hire. And if it was, I wouldn't work for you."

Clint turned to leave and McCoy said, "Hold it. Nobody walks out on me!"

Without turning Clint called back, "Mark me down as the exception to that rule too, McCoy."

McCoy, incensed, leapt out of his chair and came around from behind his desk. Clint was almost out the front door of the bank when McCoy appeared in the open doorway to his office.

"If you're not working for me, Adams, you're working against me!" he shouted, drawing all of the attention in the room.

The Gunsmith simply continued walking, ignoring McCoy completely, which angered the man even more.

He looked around the room, his eyes flicking from person to person, and they finally fell on the manager with the wire-frame glasses—which definitely did not answer the frightened young man's prayers.

"Get me Ransom!" McCoy barked, and slammed his door shut.

THIRTEEN

Clint went straight to the Olympia saloon and the first person he saw upon entering was Candace.

"Well, couldn't wait, could you?" she asked.

"I just came from McCoy's office, and I feel the need for a drink."

"Will you pay for it?" she asked. "After all, it will probably be a pleasure—"

He looked at her with a half-grimace, half-smile.

"You said we could discuss it later," she reminded him.

"I meant *later* later, not *now* later," he said. "Shall I get that drink myself?"

"Take a table, I'll bring it to you," she said.

"Whiskey," he said, "and a beer."

"As you wish, sir," she said, giving him a mock curtsy.

Clint went and sat at a back table, and when Candace came over with the drinks he said, "Join me."

"You'll have to buy me a drink," she said.

"Okay."

"Ah-hah," she said. "Got you!"

"Get your drink and sit down," he said.

"Yes, sir."

She hurried to the bar, got herself a beer, hurried back and sat down.

"Do we have someplace where we can drink these in private?" he asked.

"Sure," she said.

"You know my terms," he said.

"I also know you do nice things for a girl," she said. She stood up and said, "Come with me."

The meeting with McCoy had Clint wound up for some reason, maybe because he simply didn't like the man. There was one sure way he knew to unwind, and Candace was real good at it.

When they got upstairs, they didn't waste time sitting and drinking. He took her roughly, and she didn't seem to mind it one bit.

"Yes," she told him when he pulled her clothes off, and she said it again, over and over, when he mounted her and drove himself into her.

He cupped her firm buttocks and she set her heels against his, holding tightly to him while he sated himself on her. There were very few times when Clint Adams disregarded the pleasures of his bed partner, but this was one of them. Still, there was no lack of pleasure on Candace's part. She moaned and cried out his name as he plowed into her, his pace increasing as he felt the rush building up in his loins, and then he spewed his seed into her and she was crying and pleading for more, using her extraordinary muscle control to milk it from him.

Afterward they lay catching their breath, and then she got up, picked up their drinks and brought them back to bed with her.

"What happened?" she asked. "Didn't you get to talk to Mr. McCoy?"

"Oh, I talked to him, all right," Clint said. He paused long enough to down the whiskey and sip the beer right after it.

"Did he make his offer?"

"Did he tell you that he wanted to offer me a job?" he asked.

"No," she said, "but I know who you are, and I know that he wanted to talk to you, and I may be a whore, but at least I can put two and two together, and come out with four."

"Yeah," he said, sipping his beer. "I didn't give him a chance to make his offer. I told him I'd never work for a man like him."

"You made an enemy," she said, "and a bad one."

"I know," he said, and that's what bothered him. It was as if he went into McCoy's office with the express purpose of making an enemy of the man—and he'd succeeded. Now McCoy would most likely let Ransom loose, and Clint would have to kill the man, but would that end it?

Not likely.

"My problem is," he went on, "I've seen too many men like McCoy to just mount up and ride out in good conscience. Those people on the mountain, they're just trying to make a living. McCoy, he's trying to make other people's livings his."

"You've got that right," she said. "Are you gonna go up against him?"

"Why?" he asked. "Would you like to see me do it?"

"I'd like to see somebody take him down a few pegs," she said. "You're probably the man who could do it."

Shaking his head he said, "I don't like buying into other people's battles." The unintentional pun contained in that statement never occurred to him.

Candace put her beer mug down on the night table and leaned over him, pressing her breasts into his chest.

"Clint, when you didn't buy in on McCoy's side, you bought into the other side, the side of the mountain people."

"Are you warning me about something, Candace?" he asked.

"Just that there's nothing you can do to change that, unless you change your mind and take McCoy's offer . . . or leave town."

"And I can't do either," he said, sounding bitter.

"Why not?"

"Because I have a reputation," he explained, "and like it or not, I've got to live with it."

"Live up to it?"

"No," he said, "not up to it, just with it."

The pressure of her large breasts on his chest, the feel of her nipples, was getting him ready again, and she knew it. She reached down beneath the sheet and took hold of his semi-erect penis and stroked it to throbbing fullness.

"Now," she said, sliding down so she could take him into her mouth.

"Candace," he said as she began to suck on him, holding his cock around the base with her thumb and forefinger. He cupped the back of her head and moved his hips in unison with the tempo of her eager mouth.

"I want it all," she said, letting him slide from her mouth momentarily.

"You keep that up," he said, "and you'll get it."

She kept it up, and got all she wanted. . . .

Later, he finished the lukewarm beer, got up and got

dressed. From the bed, looking ready for more with the sheet around her waist and her breasts heaving, Candace watched him strap on his gun.

"Sure you don't want to stay awhile longer?" she asked.

"I've got to go," he said. "Thanks for the drink."

"Where are you going now?" she asked as he headed for the door.

"I'm going logging."

FOURTEEN

Clint went back to the hotel, collected his gear, and checked out. After that he went to the livery stable and paid the liveryman a lot of extra money to watch his rig and team. Sometimes the goddamn rig wasn't worth the extra worry, like now. What if McCoy decided to grab it and hold it? Everything he owned was on his back, in his saddlebags and in the rig. If he didn't want to keep worrying about the damned rig, he was going to have to stop buying into other people's fights.

After that he saddled Duke and mounted up. "We're going up the mountain, big fella. I don't know if we're doing the right thing, but if we're lucky, we'll learn something new. At least that might make the trip worth it."

He led Duke out onto the main street, and then headed for the mountain.

Deacon Platt was back in position, and when he saw the Gunsmith riding back up Main Street, he abandoned his chair and backed into a doorway again.

He watched the Gunsmith long enough to determine

60

that he was going back up the mountain, and then left his position to tell Ransom.

He was glad that Clint Adams hadn't ridden the other way out of town, which would have meant he was leaving.

He still had a chance to see the man in action.

"Mr. McCoy," Ransom said, walking into the man's office.

"Goddamn it, Ransom!" McCoy snapped angrily. "The next time you come into my office without knocking I'll have your hide!"

Ransom's back stiffened. He had taken a lot of crap from McCoy because of all the money the man was paying him, but it would be remarkably easy to draw his gun and shoot the bastard dead right where he sat.

He didn't.

"Yes, sir," he said.

"What have you got on Adams?"

"According to Piatt, Adams has started back up the mountain," Ransom said.

"Then he's a dead man," McCoy said.

When Ransom left McCoy's office, his annoyance with the man was forgotten. His hand was itching and he held it up in front of him and spoke to it.

"It looks like we're gonna get a lot more than just money out of this job," he said. He was oblivious of the looks he was getting from the employees in the bank. "A hell of a lot more."

He dropped his hand to his side and began to walk through the back to the front door. Now he was aware that people were looking at him, but that was okay.

Pretty soon they'd be looking at him differently, and with respect.

And fear . . . when he was the man who had killed the Gunsmith.

FIFTEEN

When Clint reached the top of the mountain he found somebody to lead Duke away, after explaining what he wanted done with the big fella.

"I'll check on him later," he said.

After that, he went looking for the first Battles he could find, hoping that it would be Terry.

And it was.

"You're back," she said.

"Now I know what you do around here," he said.

"What?"

"State the obvious," he replied.

She frowned at him and he said, "Sorry, that was a poor attempt at humor."

"We're not in a very humorous mood up here," she informed him.

"Well, to tell you the truth, neither am I," he said. "You tell me your reason, and I'll tell you mine."

"McCoy," she said.

He nodded. "Yep, same here." He told her about his meeting with McCoy, and he wasn't any more satisfied with it the second time through than he was the first.

"What's got you so riled up now?" he asked.

"Somebody—guess who?—busted up one of our chutes, and we've got to reassemble it."

"What's a chute?"

"It's a dry trough made of wooden planks. We use it to slide the timber down the mountain to the lake."

"And McCoy's men busted it up?"

She nodded.

"It will take us the better part of the day to repair it," she said, "putting us that much further behind schedule."

"Where are your brothers?"

"They're over by the chute supervising the repairs."

"Doesn't your brother put someone on guard duty at night?" he asked.

"What for?" she asked. "This is a mountain, not a fort. There are no Indians out there."

Clint started shaking his head slowly.

"What are you shaking your head about?" she demanded.

"If you and your brothers want to get this job done, you're going to have to change your way of thinking," he said. "You have to forget the way you're used to doing things and start behaving like you're in a war."

"A war?"

"With McCoy and his men."

"We're loggers, Clint, not soldiers," she said. "What do we know about fighting a war?"

"If that's the case," he said, shaking his head again, "this is likely to be one short war."

"You're right," she said after a moment, "unless you decide to help us."

The Gunsmith started to frown, but decided that the situation called for a scowl, instead. "Yeah," he said, kicking the dirt, "there is that, isn't there?"

SIXTEEN

When Tod Battles saw his sister Terry approaching with the Gunsmith in tow, he leaned over and tapped his brother on the arm. Big Tim turned and looked at his brother, then turned farther to look behind him.

"Clint," he said. He cast a glance at the men working on the chute, then turned and walked toward Clint and Terry. "Came back sooner than I expected."

"Sooner than I expected, too," Clint said.

"I'm afraid Tod and I won't have much time to show you around," he apologized. "Not until we get this chute repaired."

"That's no problem," Clint said. "Terry can take me around. All I need from you and your brother is some of your time later on, maybe after dinner."

"Sure," Tim said, "but what for?"

"Clint has decided to help us," Terry said.

"Oh, yeah?" Tim said. "What made up your mind for you?"

"I don't like McCoy," he said, "and I'm a sucker for long odds."

"We're bucking the long odds, huh?" Tod asked with a gleam in his eye.

"One look at that chute answers that question," Clint said, "and it could have—and should have—been avoided."

"How?" Tim asked.

"That's what we're going to talk about later, after dinner," Clint said. "For now, have somebody watching the mountain approach from town at all times."

"What for?" Tod asked.

Clint looked at him, then looked at Terry and said, "This might even be harder than I thought." He looked at Tod again and said, "Just do it."

Tod looked at his brother, who nodded and said, "Go ahead."

Tod nodded, and left to take care of it.

"Terry, show Clint around," Tim said. "One thing we should get straight even before we talk," he said to Clint then.

"What's that?"

"Who's in charge up here," Tim said. "I appreciate your help and all, but up here there can only be one boss."

"I thought the three of you were equal."

"Equal ownership, yes," Tim said, "but I run the operation. The men know who's in charge, and the last thing I'd want to do is confuse them."

The two men exchanged stares for a few moments, while Terry alternated between looking at the two.

"Well," Clint said, "I'll tell you what. I'll just be sort of an adviser. How's that?"

"That suits me," Tim said, and then after a moment's hesitation he looked at Terry, who nodded.

"Now," Clint continued, "just so the men don't go getting all confused, maybe you'd better put me on the payroll."

"I thought you were offering—" Terry began, looking confused herself now, but Tim cut her off.

"You want to be paid for helping us?"

"Just so the men won't be confused as to what my position is," Clint said.

"I see," Tim said. *If Clint Adams had been looking for a paying job, why hadn't he just come out with it in the first place?*

"And how much do you think you're worth?" Tim asked. "As an adviser, that is."

"Well, a good adviser usually earns top dollar," Clint Adams said, "so that's what I want."

"What?" Big Tim asked. "How much is that?"

"I told you," Clint said, taking Terry by the elbow, "top dollar."

He turned and propelled Terry ahead of him, and then turned back to Tim Battles and said, "Just a dollar."

SEVENTEEN

From then until dinner call Terry walked Clint around the operation, showing and explaining to him the different jobs, and logger's lingo that went with them.

First of all, he found out that a *faller* was simply the man with whom the whole logging process started, the one who cut down the tree.

A *high climber* was a man who climbed to the top of a tree to *top* it, that is, to cut off the top.

A *back cut* was the final cut made in order to cause a tree to fall.

A *bucker* was a man who trimmed the fallen trees into manageable lengths. A *peeler* trimmed the bark off the fallen tree.

The *chute*, which had already been explained to him, was one way of getting the cut tree down off the mountainside. Another way was a *skidroad*, which was a road or a path over which the logs were dragged. The road was formed out of wood, and was greased by a *skid greaser* so that the logs would slide over it more easily. The logs were pulled by a *steam donkey*, a

69

portable steam engine equipped with cables and a re-
volving drum.

"Then there are the *timber beasts*," she said at one
point during his tour.

"What the hell are those?" he asked. "Wolves?"

"No," she said with a wry smile. "We're all timber
beasts. That's what we call someone who works in the
woods." She looked at him and added, "That makes
you a timber beast now too."

"Well," he said, "I've been called a lot of things in
my time. . . ."

A little later they stopped to watch a man climb to the
top of a particularly high tree.

"Jesus," Clint breathed, watching almost in awe.

"That's Hogan," she said, "our best high
climber."

"Look at him go."

"He's got a belt tied around him and the tree," she
said, "which he uses to scale it."

"What's he got on his feet," Clint asked, shading
his eyes, "spurs?"

She started to shake her head, but then said, "I guess
you could call them that."

They watched awhile longer and then Clint heard
someone nearby who was also watching say, "Hell,
that one is a real widowmaker."

Clint looked at Terry and she said, "Ordinarily a
widowmaker is just a limb or branch that's hanging,
ready to fall on someone's head, but one of those
topped trees has been known to spin a bit on its way
down, creating a few widows of its own."

"I see."

"Do you want to watch while he finishes?" she
asked.

"Not particularly."

"Let's go down to the river, then," she said, and led the way.

When they reached the river Clint was surprised to see the water filled with floating logs. Behind them was what looked like a dam.

"What's that?" he asked.

"A splash dam," she said. "When we're ready to start the logs downriver to the mill, we'll open it up and there'll be enough of a head to drive them downstream."

"Uh-huh," he said, looking around. "There's a lot more to this business than meets the eye at first, I see."

"I guess that could be true of anyone's business," she said, looking at him closely.

"Jobs," he said, "and reputations. Is that what you're thinking?"

"Yes," she said. "Why did you agree to help us and then ask for a dollar as payment? You could have asked for more."

"And gotten it?"

"Probably."

"Damn," he said, "why didn't you tell me that before?"

"Come on," she said, "you don't get out of answering that easily. Why?"

"If the men know I'm on the payroll, they won't wonder about me so much."

"So why a dollar?" she asked. "That's like working for nothing."

He paused a moment, then placed his hand alongside her strong jaw and said, "What would you say if I told you that you were the reason?"

"I'd probably say you were a liar," she said.

He dropped his hand and asked, "Do you think all men are liars?"

"Most of them," she said. "A lot of them can't help it, and a lot of them don't want to."

"Which am I?"

"I haven't decided yet," she said, "but try another whopper like that on me and I'll let you know."

He wanted to tell her that he wasn't lying, that she was at least part of the reason he was staying, but decided against it.

"Shall we go back up?" she asked. "It'll be getting dark soon and it's almost time for dinner."

"All right," he said, "but there's still one question you haven't answered yet."

"What's that?"

"What the hell are *river pigs*?"

She laughed and then pointed to the men who were out on the river, working the logs.

"Those are river pigs, Clint," she said. "The men who work the river."

"Well, hell," he said, "couldn't anyone think of something nicer to call them?"

"Why?" she asked. "A name is just a name, something to call somebody. They don't mind."

"A name's just a name, huh?"

"Yes."

"And they don't mind?"

"That's right."

"Tell me something, then," he said.

"What?"

"Do you mind what you're called?"

"No."

"—Teresa?"

He was sure she was giving him a dirty look as he started up the mountain for dinner.

"Sentries?" Tim Battles asked.

"Day and night," Clint Adams said. "Terry said this was a mountain, not a fort, but we're going to change that right now," he added. "From now on this should be known as Fort Battles—at least, that's my advice."

"We'll take it," Tim said. "Tod and I will work out who the sentries will be."

"How many men you have working up here?"

"We had more," Tim said, "but we've still got upwards of forty."

"Well, you better divide the sentry duty into six-hour shifts, since most of these fellas aren't used to it. It's mighty boring work."

"Boring?" Tim Battles asked. He pushed away his empty plate and asked, "You ever been a peeler?"

"Uh, I can't say that I have," Clint answered. "No."

"Now that," Big Tim Battles said, "is one boring job."

As Tim Battles got up from the table and started out of the mess hall Clint leaned over to Terry and asked, "With all the funny names you people throw around up here, what do you call him?"

"Tim?" she asked, looking after her massive brother. "He's the big boss around here, Clint. We refer to him as 'the bull of the woods.' "

"Son of a bitch," Clint said, watching Big Tim Battles squeeze through the doorway, "you finally came up with one that makes sense."

EIGHTEEN

Bennett Ransom, following McCoy's instructions—McCoy called them orders, but Ransom always called them instructions—rounded up Deacon Platt and three other men and brought them all back to McCoy's office after banking hours.

"Don't anyone sit down," McCoy said. "You won't be here that long."

They all looked at each other, except Ransom. Ever since he realized that he was going to be the man who killed the Gunsmith, he had been trying to assert himself in McCoy's presence. He stared at McCoy now, waiting for the man to give his latest instructions.

"I understand that breaking up one of the Battleses' chutes didn't slow them down significantly."

"Huh?" Deacon Platt said, frowning.

Ransom, ignoring Platt, said, "It slowed them down at least a day."

"That's not enough," McCoy said. "We've got to come up with something else. Anybody got any ideas?"

He looked around at the blank faces and wondered why he had asked that question. These five men probably couldn't scare up an idea between them.

"I didn't think so," he said.

"Wait—" Ransom started, but McCoy continued on as if he hadn't heard the man.

"I think more drastic measures are necessary," McCoy said.

"Like what?" Ransom asked.

"Ransom, take some men up to that camp and raise some hell," McCoy said.

"How do you suggest I do that?"

"I don't know," McCoy said. "Why don't you try burning something down?"

"Like what?"

"Ransom, there's plenty of wood up there," McCoy told him. "Pick something out."

"And what happens if we're recognized and traced right back to you?"

"You won't be."

"What makes you so sure?" Ransom asked. McCoy looked sharply at the gunman, because he thought that there was a hint of challenge in the man's questions all of a sudden.

"Ransom," McCoy said, "I am sure of what I'm doing in all of my business dealings. This one's no different."

Ransom backed off a bit and said, "Well, I'd still like to know how we're gonna charge on up there and set a fire without being recognized."

"It'll be dark, Ransom," McCoy said.

"Not when we light them fires," Platt offered, feeling pretty proud of his cleverness—until both McCoy and Ransom stared at him hard.

"It'll be dark," McCoy said, "and you'll be wearing these."

He took something out of his desk and tossed it to

Ransom. It was a piece of black cloth, a mask with eyeholes cut into it, and nothing more.

"All right," Ransom said, "so we wear hoods. Who do you think they're gonna suspect after we get finished?"

"What they suspect doesn't mean a thing," McCoy said. "The only thing that would carry any weight is what they can prove, and they're not going to be able to prove a damned thing."

Ransom had to admit that McCoy seemed to have all the angles figured.

"Okay, boys," he said, "let's get going."

They started for the door and McCoy called out, "Ransom."

"Yeah?"

McCoy noticed that Ransom had stopped saying, "Yes, sir," but let it pass.

"If you should happen to come across the Gunsmith while you're up there," the banker said, "kill him."

"Yes, sir!" Ransom said, and closed the door firmly on the way out.

NINETEEN

The full moon, coupled with the sentry Clint "suggested" be posted, saved Battles Mountain that night.

The sentry was a faller named Anton O'Toole, whose mother was French and father was Irish. It was a combination that caused him not to know what he liked better—a good woman or a good, drunken brawl.

What he didn't like was being on sentry duty that night, instead of in town at the Olympia Whorehouse—which also happened to be owned by McCoy.

"Just what I don't need," he muttered to himself with just the hint of an Irish accent, "to be babysitting a bunch of trees when my own root is as hard as one." With his right hand he pressed down on his "root," which had been ready for a trip to town since afternoon.

"*Merde,*" he said, using one of the few French words he had learned from his mother, and still remembered.

He fidgeted restlessly on the tree stump he was sitting on, looking up at the full moon. When he looked back down the mountain he thought for a moment that he might have seen something, but after a few moments, he convinced himself that he was mistaken.

He looked down at the old Navy Colt one of the other men had given him when Big Tim ordered that he'd have to be armed while standing sentry duty—like he was in the damned army, or something. Trees he knew plenty about, but he didn't know shit about guns.

He only hoped he didn't accidentally shoot off his foot—or his rigid root!

Bennett Ransom was leading five men, including Deacon Platt, up the mountain on foot.

"How much farther—" Platt started to ask, because he had never been up to the camp before, but Ransom cut him off with a violent motion of his hand.

"Shut up," he hissed. "Sound carries at night."

Platt shut his mouth tight and continued to follow closely behind Ransom. He wished he could take off his hood, or that McCoy had at least given them hoods with a nose hole as well as two eye holes. He kept lifting the hood up over his nose to take a deep breath, and then dropping it down again. He also had a mustache, which didn't make it any more comfortable.

Each of the six men were carrying torches which were not as yet lit, and Ransom was carrying some lucifer matches. When the time came he would light each man's torch, and they would touch off anything that would burn—including trees.

Ransom was glad that the action had finally started. Busting up the chute and delaying supplies was never the way he would have done things. He would have broken a few bones right at the beginning, or even out and out killed some of Tim Battles's best loggers. That's what McCoy should have let him do if he was really serious about taking the mountain. Obviously, McCoy didn't have the guts to go that far until everything else failed.

What Ransom especially liked was the go-ahead to kill the Gunsmith if he had the opportunity. He wasn't going to wait for that eventuality, however. He was going to make that opportunity, take advantage of it, and kill Clint Adams.

He was going to leave Olympia with a lot of money in his pocket—and the Gunsmith's reputation.

Clint went to sleep in the same bed he had used the night before, and lay awake for a while. He thought about McCoy, he thought about the whore, Candace, and he thought a lot about Teresa Battles.

Clint Adams's own root wasn't exactly dormant when he finally fell asleep.

Terry Battles, sleeping in the hut she shared with her brothers, was thinking about Clint Adams in a way she had thought about few men before. Tod Battles, earlier that evening, had teased his sister a bit about the way she had been looking at Clint, and she had snapped at him testily which, she realized, was tantamount to admitting that yes, she was beginning to have ''woman thoughts''—as Tod called them—about Clint Adams.

And it bothered her.

Big Tim Battles's only thoughts as he drifted off to sleep were about how to save his mountain. He only hoped that hiring the Gunsmith was a step in the right direction.

●   ●   ●

McCoy, safe and sound in his house on the south edge of town, was waiting patiently to hear that things had gone as planned on the mountain.

Contrary to Ransom's way of thinking, McCoy had no qualms about killing, he simply knew that it was smart to keep it as the last resort. For instance, the first thing he would do once he had possession of Big Tim Battles's mountain would be to kill Bennett Ransom.

It was infinitely preferable to paying him the exorbitant amount of money they had agreed on.

It occurred to him that it may have been a good thing that Clint Adams had not accepted his offer. It would undoubtedly be easier to kill a Bennett Ransom than it would be to kill the Gunsmith.

Contrary to what a Bennett Ransom might think.

Anton O'Toole picked up the Navy Colt and hefted it, and decided if felt pretty good in his meaty hand. He wondered how long those legendary gunfighters like Wild Bill Hickok and Wyatt Earp had had to practice with their pistol until they became so good.

He held it out in front of him, sighting down the barrel at some imaginary opponent, and pretended to fire a shot.

"Pow," he said. The fact of the matter was that Anton O'Toole had never fired a gun in his life, and he was curious about it now that he had a gun in his hand.

Wouldn't it be funny, he thought, *to fire a shot and wake up the whole camp?*

As he sighted down the barrel again he thought he saw something farther on down the incline.

A flash of some kind of light?

He peered into the darkness, holding the gun down

by his side now, with his finger unconsciously curled around the trigger.

"Are we close enough?" Deacon Platt asked.

"Damn it," Ransom hissed at him. He turned to look at Platt and saw that the man had pulled his hood up over his mouth, which further angered him.

"Pull that down."

Platt's fingers spasmodically pulled at the mask cloth, yanking it down over his mouth.

"We're close enough," Ransom said. He could see the structures of the mess hall, the bunkhouse, and the Battleses' hut. What he did not see was what he did not expect to see—Anton O'Toole, the lone sentry who was sitting off to the left of their line of vision. In plain sight, if they had chosen to look at him.

Ransom took a lucifer from his pocket and said, "Hold out your torches."

Before striking the match he gave each man his orders. Two of them were to set fire to the bunkhouse, two would torch the mess hall, and Platt and himself would set fire to the hut.

"Have you all got that?"

Five black hooded heads nodded in unison.

Ransom flicked his nail against the lucifer, and it flared to life.

This was the small flash of light that Anton O'Toole thought he saw.

O'Toole saw a large flash of light, followed closely by another and another . . .

Fire! he thought. Fire was the one thing that could totally wipe out a logging operation.

Fire! he thought again, and in a blind panic, his finger cocked the hammer and jerked on the trigger of the Navy Colt, firing it into the ground.

TWENTY

The Gunsmith's body reacted to the sound of the shock before his mind did. His thoughts were still fuzzy even as he lurched to his feet, clawing for his gun. He was the first man out of the bunkhouse, clad only in his pants, and heard Anton O'Toole shout "Fire," just before the man was cut down by a bullet from Bennett Ransom's gun.

That second shot aroused the remainder of the camp.

"Go," Ransom snapped to his men, and they began to run forward, carrying their burning torches.

Ransom started running with Deacon Platt towards the small hut, but stopped as he spotted Clint Adams, standing shirtless in the moonlight.

This was his chance, he thought, but as he raised his gun to fire, the rest of the men from the bunkhouse exploded from the door, and Clint Adams was momentarily lost in the crowd.

"Damn!" Ransom cursed, and continued on towards the hut.

"What the hell—" Big Tim Battles shouted as he burst from the small structure. He saw a hooded man approaching with a lighted torch, and ran to intercept him. The man, however, had gotten as close as need be and threw the torch so that it landed on the roof of the hut.

"Tim—" Tod shouted, coming out behind his brother.

"Get on the roof," Tim shouted to his younger brother. "Fire!"

As the big logger closed ground on the hooded man, the smaller man began to turn to run. As he did so, Tim Battles threw himself at the man, striking him in the small of the back with his shoulder and sending him sprawling.

Aware that they could not afford to have even one of their number unmasked, Bennett Ransom calmly fired a shot at the logging camp leader as he began to rise to his feet. The bullet smacked into Battles's massive shoulder, throwing him back onto the ground.

Ransom ran towards Platt and, using one hand, lifted the man back to his feet.

"Get out of here," he told him, and Platt took off.

Ransom prepared to fire another shot at the fallen logger when a bullet kicked up dust at his feet. As he looked to see who was firing at him, a second bullet came closer, and he decided to back off.

The shots were being fired by Terry Battles, who had rushed from the hut gun in hand. The only woman in camp, she was the only one who had paused to dress before responding to the shouts and gunshots. Because of this, she was able to save her brother's life.

Clint Adams saw the two hooded men bearing torches running towards the bunkhouse and knew what they had in mind. He snapped off a shot that caught one of the men on the left hip, spinning him around and causing his torch to fall into the dirt. His partner stopped, threw his torch towards the bunkhouse, and dragged the other man away. His torch fell far short of its mark.

The two men who were running towards the mess hall were intercepted and almost trampled by a large group of loggers. Their torches were stamped out on the ground, but in their haste to do the same to the two men carrying them, the loggers got in each other's way and allowed the two men to escape.

"Water, I need water," Tod Battles shouted from the roof of the burning hut, and the hooded men were forgotten in favor of trying to put the fire out.

As the loggers rushed to Tod's assistance, Clint spotted Terry Battles with her gun in her hand, crouched over her brother, as if to physically shield him from further bullets. He saw that Tim was alive, and went first to check on Anton O'Toole, the man who had warned them all. After that, he ran over to Terry and Big Tim.

"He's been shot," Terry said to him as he reached them. "He won't stay down."

"Let me up, damn it!" Tim was yelling, but his sister kept her big body leaning on his, hindering his attempts towards getting to his feet.

"Stay down," Clint said. He put his hand on Tim's uninjured shoulder and pushed him down to the ground. "Let me have a look."

"What about the fires?" Tim demanded.

"There's only one, and it's being handled by Tod and the others," Clint said. "Sit still, damn it, you've got a hole in you big enough for my fist to fit in."

"Then stuff it in and stop the bleeding, damn you," Tim snapped back, but he had ceased his efforts to get to his feet and his face was ashen, betraying the pain he was in.

"What can we do?" Terry demanded, waving the hand with which she was holding her gun, a .45 way too big for her.

"For starters you can put that cannon down before it goes off," Clint said.

"It won't go off unless I want it to," she assured him, but stuck it in her belt.

"We've got to stop this hole up with something, and then either get him to a doctor, or get the doc up here."

"It would probably be faster to take him down to town," Terry said, regaining her composure. "We can take him down in a steam donkey."

"No," Tim said immediately. "We need that up here. Just sit me on a horse."

Terry looked at Clint, who was stuffing torn pieces of Tim's nightshirt into his wound and said, "He can't sit a horse with this hole in him."

"One of the other wagons, then," Tim broke in, "but not the steam donkey."

"All right," Terry said. She looked at Clint and said, "You and I will take him."

"No," Tim said tightly, grimacing against the pain, "not you, Terry. You've got to stay—"

Terry looked over at Tod, who was on the ground now, shouting orders, and said, "Tod can handle it, Tim. He's ready."

"Agh," Tim said, surrendering finally to the immense pain he was feeling. "All right, all right. Get me some whiskey, damn it, Terry!"

She looked at Clint and he nodded to her and said, "Make it a full bottle. He's going to need it."

TWENTY-ONE

The trip down the mountain road was not an easy one for Big Tim Battles. They cushioned the buckboard as much as they could, and made him as comfortable as possible. Terry sat in the back with him, trying to minimize the damage a bump would do to his wound, while Clint drove. Duke trailed along behind them.

They reached town before dawn and woke the doctor from his sound sleep.

"Take him into my office," the elderly sawbones said. His name was Dr. Palance, and he was used to such rude awakenings.

Terry and Clint waited in the doctor's outer office while he tended to Tim in his examining room.

"How bad was his wound?" she asked Clint.

"It was a big hole," Clint admitted, "but then what other size wound would a big man like your brother have?"

She still had the .45 tucked into her belt and Clint said, "You saved his life."

"Don't tell *him* that," she said, touching the butt of her gun. "I was supposed to have gotten rid of this long ago, but I hid it."

"You should have one that better suits your hand," he said. "That's too big for you."

"It doesn't much matter," she said. "I don't usually hit anything anyways."

"If you're going to own a gun," he said, "you should know how to use it."

She nodded, but it was more from tiredness than in agreement with what he'd said.

"Let me get you a hotel room, Terry," he said. "You need to get some sleep."

"Not yet," she said. "I want to see how my brother is."

"I'll wait and let you know."

"You can take a room if you want," she said, "but I won't use it until I know how Tim is."

"I'll get you a room," he said, shaking his head at her stubbornness.

He walked to the hotel, took a room for her, and when he returned to the doctor's office he found her asleep in her chair. At that moment, the door of the examining room opened and the doctor came out.

"How is he?" she asked, snapping her eyes open.

"He's got a big hole in him," the doctor said, "but I got the bullet out. He'll be fine, but he'll have to rest."

"He will," Terry said, "if I have to sit on him. Can we take him back?"

"Up the mountain?" Doc Palance asked, raising his eyebrows. "Not advisable, young lady."

"He'll insist on going back," she said.

"Keep him in town for at least a day," the doctor

said. "I want to make sure there's no infection. He can stay right where he is, if you like, until tomorrow."

"We're grateful," she said.

"You'd better get some sleep yourself, Miss Battles," the doctor advised. "You look like you're just about out on your feet."

"She'll get some sleep, doc," Clint said, and then looking directly into Terry's eyes he added, "if I have to sit on her myself."

Clint walked Terry to the hotel, where they got her key from the clerk.

"Do you want a room too, sir?" the clerk asked.

"No."

The clerk smirked at that, and Clint resisted his impulse to smack the look from the man's face.

He led the weary woman up the steps to her room, opened the door for her and ushered her inside.

She sat heavily on the bed, shoulders slumped.

"Sometimes I wonder if the effort is worth it," she said.

"That doesn't sound like you," Clint said.

She looked up at him and said, "No, it doesn't, does it? I'm a Battles, like my brothers. I'm supposed to be stubborn, and confident, even if it means being reckless as well."

He walked to her and laid his hand alongside the left side of her jaw.

"You are a Battles," he said softly, "but not at all like your brothers."

She looked up at him and at that moment, with her face resting in his hand, he thought she had never looked lovelier.

"I'll wake you if there's any change in Tim's condition," he said.

"No," she replied, grabbing him by the wrist. She stared boldly into his eyes and said, "Stay with me."

He stared back at her, and then said, "Yes."

TWENTY-TWO

He placed his other hand on the other side of her face, cupped it, and leaned over to kiss her generous lips. When her mouth opened eagerly to his, it was as sweet as he had imagined it would be.

He slid his hands down to her shoulders, and then to the buttons of her shirt. The kiss continued as he undid all of her buttons and slid the shirt off. In her haste to dress and join the fracas on the mountain, she had not put on any underclothes, which was just as well. Clint was too impatient to have dealt with them.

He slid his hands to the undersides of her full breasts and cupped one in each hand, enjoying the smoothness of her skin against his hand. She shuddered as his lips moved to her shoulders.

Terry barely breathed as he rubbed his palms over her nipples, causing them to swell and harden. Next, he lowered himself to his knees, so that he could caress her nipples with his tongue and lips, and she shuddered again.

"Clint," she said.

"Hmm?"

"I want to feel like a woman," she said, softly. "Make me feel like a woman."

"You are a woman," he said, kissing the soft hollow of her throat. "There can be no doubt about that in your mind, or any man's mind."

He kissed her then, and she clutched the back of his head in her hands, winding her fingers in the thick strands, darting her tongue into his mouth.

"Make love to me," she implored against his mouth.

He pushed her down on the bed and finished undressing her. Then he stood and undressed while she watched him.

When he joined her on the bed, covering her lush body with his taut, lean body, she wrapped her arms around him and said into his ear, "You're a beautiful man."

"Oh, yes?" he said.

"No, really," she said, reaching between them so she could close her fist around his rigidness, "a beautiful, beautiful man. I've never seen a beautiful man before."

"Shh," he said, kissing her to silence her.

He rubbed his rock-hard cock against her pubic patch, enjoying the sensations that the wiry strands caused as they tickled the tender underside of his penis. He could feel her wetness, and he knew she was ready for him.

"I want to go slowly," he told her. "I want to make this last."

"I'll do whatever you want," she said, shuddering again in response to his touch. "It's been so long since I've had a man," she added, and then qualified the remark by saying, "It's been a long time since I've seen one I wanted."

"I'm honored," he said.

"You should be," she replied, licking his lips.

He moved his hips against hers, but he did not allow himself to enter her just yet.

She lifted her hips to meet him, thinking that he was going to enter, and when he didn't she bit his lower lip and whispered, "Bastard."

"I told you I want this to last," he said.

"Fuck me, you bastard," she hissed. She grabbed him by the buttocks and forced him to enter her in one swift movement, which brought a moan from deep inside of her.

"Oh, God."

"See," he said, "I told you I wanted to go slow, but no . . ."

"Shut up and fuck," she said, lifting her hips up off the bed again.

"All right, lady," he said.

He slid his hands beneath her to cup her buttocks, and then drove himself into her hard, squeezing the cheeks of her behind hard enough to leave the imprint of his fingers in bruises.

"Too hard?" he asked as he rammed into her again.

"Oh, harder, Clint, do it harder—"

She wrapped her legs around his waist and for a moment he thought she was going to break his back. Damn, but she was strong!

"Oh, Jesus, yes," she moaned. "Oh sweet Jesus, that's it, keep doing it . . ."

She began to whip her head back and forth on the pillow as her body trembled with her first orgasm.

The sweat was beaded on her upper lip and he ran his tongue along it.

"You didn't . . ." she said, wriggling her hips.

"Not yet," he said, although he didn't tell her what

an effort it had been to hold back.

"How long—" she started to ask him, but he answered before she could get the question out.

"As long as you can," he said, grinning wolfishly at her.

"That sounds like a challenge," she said.

It was, he thought, and it was also a surefire way to keep her mind off her brother . . . and his mind, as well.

"I'd like to get on top," she said then.

"Be my guest," he said.

Working together they managed to turn the double-backed animal over and she sat astride him, staring down into his eyes while he reached up and massaged her breasts.

"Oh my God," she said, "that feels good."

"Where?"

"All over," she said. "Damn you, Clint Adams, but you are so good."

"You're not so bad yourself," he replied, "for someone who claims to be out of practice."

"Claims?" she demanded, reaching behind her to take his balls in her hand.

"Hold it, hold it," he said.

"That's what I'm doing," she pointed out, smiling lewdly.

"Yeah, but if you don't squeeze, I promise I'll show you a trick."

"What kind of trick?" she asked, curiously.

"Let go first."

"All right," she said, "but remember, I'm in the dominant position."

That's what you say, he thought.

"Okay, so now what?" she asked. She was still

seated astride him with the long, hard length of him comfortably nestled inside of her.

"Lean down here," he said.

She hesitated, eyeing him suspiciously, but then leaned over so that her large, pendulous breasts were dangling in his face. He put one hand on each side, squeezed her breasts together, and then began to suck and lick both of her swollen nipples at the same time.

"Oh, yes," she said, moving her hips, sending waves of sensation through her insides while he continued to suck on her nipples. "Oh, that feels incredible. I didn't even know you could do that," she said, closing her eyes.

"Only if you're big enough," he said, "and you're big enough."

"Don't talk," she said, and he went back to what he was doing.

She began to ride up and down his stiff rod while he suckled her, and as her tempo increased he had to put his arms around her to hold her torso as still as possible.

"Oh, yes," she said again, "suck them, suck them hard—ooh, bite them . . ."

As she urged him on, she continued to ride his swollen cock up and down until finally he felt her spasms again.

"Ohh," she said as the spasms decreased. She moved her hips then and felt that he was still hard and ready.

"Enough," she said.

"You've had enough?" he asked.

"No, I mean I haven't had enough," she said. "I want you to come, too. Let's turn over again."

Actually, he was ready for that too. His cock was aching to explode inside her and fill her up. They executed their previous move again, turning over without breaking their connection, and then she said, "Now, Clint, do it now."

He began to take her in long, hard strokes then, and it wasn't long before he built his head of steam to the point of exploding.

"Oh, I feel you, I feel you," she said, "you're ready . . . you're coming . . ."

And he was, in hard, powerful spurts that felt so good it was almost painful. He moaned aloud as she locked her legs around him and began to grind her pelvis, milking all she could get from him.

"Uh," she panted, yanking on him violently with the muscles of her cunt.

"Terry," he said, "that's all there is."

"Mmm," she said, pulling his face down to her so that she could kiss him hungrily, sucking furiously on his tongue.

"Is that really all there is, Clint?" she asked then, reaching behind him to tease his sac.

"Well," he said, outlining her full mouth with the tip of his tongue, "for a little while, anyway."

A very little while.

TWENTY-THREE

"How much damage did you do?" McCoy demanded.

Ransom fidgeted, moving his weight from foot to foot beneath the banker's angry glare.

"Uh, I'm not sure," he said. He wished some of the others were there to take a little of the heat as well, but they were off getting the wounded man cared for . . . without going to Doc Palance.

"Nothing should have gone wrong, Ransom," McCoy said. "Nothing!" He slammed a meaty fist down on top of his desk to bring his point home. "So how did it?"

"They were ready for us," Ransom said.

"How?"

"I don't know," the gunman said. "Who expected them to have a lookout posted?"

"A lookout?" McCoy asked. "Why didn't you get rid of the man before you made your move?"

"We didn't see him!"

"You didn't see him? I'm paying you a great deal of money, Ransom, and you didn't see the lookout?"

"We didn't expect—"

"You knew the Gunsmith was up there, didn't you?" McCoy asked, interrupting the man's attempt to defend himself.

"Sure, I knew—"

"What did you think," McCoy asked, "that he was up there for his health?"

"Look—"

"Shut up," McCoy said, shifting restlessly in his chair. "Clint Adams has made his position clear now. We are no longer dealing simply with a bunch of loggers. We've got to go about this differently."

"Tim Battles was shot," Ransom said.

"What?"

"I shot Battles."

"Why didn't you tell me that before, you idiot?"

"You didn't give me a—"

"Is he dead?"

"I don't know," Ransom said. "Platt said they brought him into town to see Doc Palance."

"Who brought him in?"

"Adams and the girl."

"Adams is in town?"

Ransom nodded.

"Maybe you should have a little meeting with the Gunsmith before he goes back up to the mountain," McCoy suggested.

"It would be my pleasure," Ransom said, rubbing his hands together.

"Ransom."

"Yeah?"

"Why are you so sure you can take him?"

"I've heard stories about him," the gunman said.

"There are a lot of stories about a lot of gunmen," McCoy said.

"These are different," Ransom said. "I've heard that he doesn't like to use his gun. That's dangerous for a man with a rep like his."

"What do you mean?"

"A man who doesn't like to use his gun will hesitate," Ransom explained, "and that will get him killed every time."

"What about you?"

"What about me?"

"Don't you ever hesitate, Ransom?"

Bennett Ransom laughed harshly, and for the first time McCoy was not quite so sure that the man would be easy to dispose of once the mountain was his.

"I never hesitate, McCoy," Ransom said. It was the first time he had not called the banker "Mr." as if he could see the germ of doubt growing in McCoy's mind.

"Why not?"

"Because I like to use my gun," Ransom said, drawing it so swiftly that McCoy could almost believe that it had simply appeared in his hand.

McCoy watched the gunman fondle his weapon, turn it over in his hand, stare at it the way most men would stare at a beautiful woman.

McCoy felt a chill, the like of which he had never felt before. He had never considered himself an evil man, just a man who knew what he wanted, and took it.

Bennett Ransom, on the other hand, was evil.

"I like to kill," Ransom said, "and killing the Gunsmith is going to be extra sweet."

TWENTY-FOUR

Later, Clint and Terry dressed and walked over to the doctor's office together. On the way, something occurred to Clint.

"I know I shot one of the men last night," he said.

"Did you kill him?"

"I don't know," he said. "They dragged him away with them. He must have been hurt at least as bad as your brother. The trip down the mountain may have killed him if I didn't."

"How do we find out?"

"*We* don't," Clint said. "I do."

"But—"

"You go into doc's and see how Tim is," Clint said, "and while you're there, check with him and see if he's treated any other gunshot wounds today."

"Where will you be?"

"I'm going to check with the undertaker, see if he's had any new clients since last night."

"Where should we meet?"

"Right back here," Clint said as they stopped in front of Doc Palance's office.

"You stopping anyplace else?"

"Who knows?" he asked with a shrug. "I might stop at the saloon for a drink and some conversation."

"Men," she said, shaking her head. "You're all alike, all little boys."

"That's not what you were saying a few hours ago," he reminded her.

"See?" she said, as if that one word served to prove her point, and she entered the doctor's office.

Clint shook his head and started for the saloon he'd first come to in Olympia.

"Well, look who's here," Cooper said as the Gunsmith entered the saloon. "Thought you left a long time ago."

"Really?" Clint asked. "Or did you think I was dead?"

"Why would I think that?" the old man asked.

"You told Ransom who I was, didn't you?" Clint asked, strictly on a hunch. Cooper looked like an old man who had been a lot of places and seen a lot of things.

"Give me a beer while you're trying to think of a good answer, Cooper," Clint said.

Cooper got the beer and when he set it down in front of Clint, the Gunsmith saw that his hand was shaking.

"I'm not Ransom, Cooper," he said, picking up his beer, "in more ways than one. I'm not looking to put a bullet between your eyes. I'm just curious about who told Ransom who I was, that's all."

For some reason, Clint Adams's calm demeanor frightened Cooper even more than Ransom's threats had.

"Yeah, it was me who told him," Cooper finally said, "but he made sure I knew what he'd do to me if I didn't tell him who you were."

"I'm sure he did, Cooper," Clint said.

"You ain't mad at me?" the old bartender asked anxiously.

"No, I'm not mad," Clint assured him.

Cooper looked visibly relieved and said, "You want another beer?"

"I haven't paid for this one yet."

"Forget it," Cooper said, "they're on me."

After the second beer Cooper gave Clint directions to the undertaker's office, and told him that the man's name was John Graves.

"He claims it's his real name," the old man had added, "but I have my doubts."

"Mr. Graves?" Clint asked as he entered.

Every undertaker Clint ever knew had always seemed to be tall and cadaverous, or short and fat. This one seemed to combine the two. The man was very tall, and obese. He had at least three chins, and his belly hung over his belt like a sack of dirty clothes.

"I'm Graves," the man replied, seeming to take great pride in the admission.

"This may seem like a strange question, Mr. Graves, but I'd like to know if you've had any business since last night."

"You mean, have I had any clients?" the man asked.

"Uh, yes, clients," Clint said.

"Why," Graves asked, "have you killed anyone?"

"Not that I know of," Clint said. At that moment an

odd thought struck him. He hadn't had a chance to stop in and introduce himself to the local lawman, and hadn't even seen a man with a badge during his stay. Even the brawl in the saloon that first day had not produced a man wearing a star.

Did Olympia have a lawman? That was a question to look into later, because it would help to know if there was a sheriff, and if so, what his relationship was with McCoy.

"I'd simply like to know if anyone has been killed since last night, that you know of," Clint said. "It seems a fairly simple question to me."

"Simple," Graves said, looking Clint up and down. "Yes. Well, if you must know, I haven't buried anyone in about a week, and that was when old Mrs. Miller's heart finally gave out."

"Nothing since then, huh?"

"Not a body," Graves said with a straight face. "It's getting hard to make a living around here."

"You have my sympathies," Clint said. "Thank you for answering my question."

"Don't mention it," the undertaker said. "From the looks of you, I figure you'll be sending me some business pretty soon."

"You can tell that just from looking at me, huh?" Clint asked, wondering if perhaps the man knew more than he was saying.

"I deal in death, mister," Graves said. "I know a man in the same business when I see one."

Clint stared at the man for a long moment. He found it strange that he was feeling no particular reaction to the man's remark.

Was that because he agreed with it?

Finally he said, "I'll see what I can do for you, Mr. Graves."

The undertaker nodded and said, "Any effort to improve my business would be greatly appreciated. A man's got to eat."

TWENTY-FIVE

When Clint left the undertaker's place—still bothered by the man's remark about "knowing a man in the same business"—he returned to the doctor's office and found Terry sitting alone.

"Where's the doc?" he asked.

"He's with Tim," she said.

"Did you ask him about any other men, injured or dead?" Clint asked.

"Yes," Terry answered. "He hasn't had any patients with gunshot wounds, and hasn't heard of any shooting deaths."

"They must be taking care of the man's wound themselves," Clint said. "Either that, or they've let him die." Another thought struck him and he asked, "Is there another doctor in town?"

"Not that I know of."

"A horse doctor, maybe?"

"Just the blacksmith. We had to use him for one of our mules, once."

"Then maybe I should have a talk with him," Clint said, half to himself. He looked up then and asked, "How's your brother?"

"The doctor was telling me that he doesn't advise that Tim make the trip up the mountain today, tomorrow, or even the day after that."

"How bad is the wound?"

"It hasn't become infected, but the doc still says that it will take the better part of a month for it to heal."

"I doubt that Big Tim Battles is the kind of man to take that information to heart."

"No, he's not. The doctor is talking to him now, but Tim is going to want to go back today."

She looked at Clint helplessly, and he stepped forward to put his hand on her shoulder.

"Then we'll take him back, Terry," he said.

She placed her hand on his wrist and said, "Thank you, Clint."

At that moment the doctor came out of his examining room and both of them dropped their hands to their sides.

"Doctor?" Terry asked.

The doctor shook his head and said, "Your brother is a very stubborn man, Miss Battles."

"I know," she said.

"It runs in the family, doc," Clint added.

"The lady tells me that you're interested in finding a man with a bullet in him. Is he the one who shot my patient?"

"No, but he was with the man who did it."

"As I told her, I haven't had any patients, and Graves, the undertaker—"

"I've spoken to him," Clint broke in.

"Charming fella, eh?" the doctor said.

"Tell me about it," Clint replied. "Doc, is there a lawman in this town?"

The doctor sighed and said, "I suppose you could call him that . . . technically. His name's Thorpe, and he's nothing but a puppet for the banker, McCoy."

The old story, Clint thought bitterly. *The man with the power buys the law*. Men had tried it enough with him when he was a lawman, and it had never worked, but there were plenty of men out there who wore a star only for what it could get them.

"Thorpe?"

"Yes, Sam Thorpe. His office is down the block a ways, but talking to him won't do you any good."

"Why doesn't somebody do something about him if he's not a good lawman?"

"Nobody else wants the job," the doc said, simply, and Clint let it stand.

"What about your patient?" Clint said. "What will the trip up the mountain do to him?"

"Kill him, likely," the doctor said, and Terry caught her breath. "I can't say I like the idea, but if you make him as comfortable as possible, minimize the bumps and don't start his wound bleeding again, he could make it."

"Then that's what we'll have to do," Clint said, looking at Terry.

"As long as you both know that I'm against it," the doctor said, "and won't accept any responsibility for the consequences."

"We understand," Terry assured him.

"When will you be leaving, then?" he asked, and Terry looked to Clint for the answer.

"In a hour," Clint said, "after I've spoken with the sheriff and that blacksmith."

"The blacksmith?" the doctor said. He nodded and

said, "Oh yes, he might be able to handle a bullet wound, if it wasn't very serious. I'll have your brother ready in an hour, miss."

"Thank you."

Clint and Terry left the doctor's office and spoke out front.

"You can go to the hotel, Terry, and get checked out. My gear is still in the livery, so pack your own and be ready to leave within the hour."

"What if you find the man you're looking for?" she asked. "The man you wounded?"

"If I find him and he leads me back to McCoy," Clint said, "then maybe Tim won't have to rush back to his mountain after all."

TWENTY-SIX

Clint stopped at the sheriff's office to meet Sheriff Sam Thorpe.

"Are you Sheriff Thorpe?" he asked as he entered the office.

The man behind the desk looked up and narrowed his eyes as he studied the Gunsmith speculatively. *He knows who I am,* Clint thought, as he studied the man right back.

Thorpe was a big, florid-faced man in his early thirties who looked competent enough upon first meeting. Clint was perfectly ready to give the man all the time he needed to show otherwise.

"I'm Thorpe," the man finally said.

"My name's Clint Adams, Sheriff," Clint said.

"I know who you are."

"Really?" Clint asked. "Now, that's strange."

"What's so strange?" Thorpe asked.

"Well, if I was the sheriff and a man with a rep came to town, I'd make it my business to check him out, see how long he was planning to stay, see whether or not he was getting into trouble or not. You couldn't possibly

109

have heard about a fracas I got into over at the saloon, could you?''

''You trying to tell me how to do my job?'' Thorpe demanded.

''No, I wouldn't do that,'' Clint said. ''Besides, I hear you've already got someone to do that for you.''

''What does that mean?'' Thorpe asked, sitting straight up in his chair.

''Nothing,'' Clint assured him. ''Just some gossip I've heard around town.''

''Who's been—''

''Actually, I've come over here to make a complaint,'' Clint said, changing the subject abruptly.

''A complaint?'' the lawman asked, cautiously. ''What about?''

''I was visiting some friends up on a mountain,'' Clint said, ''and the funniest thing happened. Somebody tried to burn the mountain down.''

''What mountain?''

''Oh, you know it,'' Clint said. ''It's the one Big Tim Battles is working on.''

''Battles,'' Thorpe said. ''Now there's a troublemaker.''

''Yeah, I know,'' Clint said. ''Last night he actually stole somebody's bullet by stepping in front of it.''

''What's that?''

''Somebody shot him, Sheriff,'' Clint said.

''Do you know who?''

''We don't have any proof, no,'' Clint said.

''Then there's nothing I can do,'' Thorpe said.

''You could investigate,'' Clint said. ''I mean, it's no secret that the banker, McCoy, is after the mountain. Maybe he sent the hooded gunmen after the Battleses, last night.''

"Hooded gunmen?" the sheriff asked. "Why would Mr. McCoy do that? He's a businessman."

"Ah, I see," Clint said.

"Besides," Thorpe said, "it's not like Battles was killed, right?"

"How did you know?"

"Know what?" Thorpe asked.

"That Battles wasn't dead?"

"Uh, you told me," the sheriff said nervously.

"No," Clint said, "I didn't. I told you he was shot, I didn't say whether he was killed or not."

"Sure you did," Thorpe insisted.

"Nope," Clint said, "I didn't."

"Was he killed?"

"No, he wasn't."

"Well then?" Thorpe said. "What's the problem?"

"You didn't seem to know about the incident at first," Clint said, "so I'm just wondering how you knew he wasn't dead, that's all."

"Well, maybe I did know," Thorpe said, trying to look sly and succeeding in looking desperate. He had given himself away and was wondering how he was going to tell McCoy.

"If you did, why aren't you doing something about it?"

"I'm . . . conducting an investigation," Thorpe said.

"Don't you think you should talk to the people involved then?" Clint asked.

Thorpe decided to tough it out and stood up.

"Look, Adams, you're trying to tell me how to do my job again," Thorpe said. "I don't like that."

"That's too bad," Clint said.

Thorpe, looking nervous, blustered, "I know your

reputation, Adams, but I'm the law in this town, whether you like it or not.''

Clint had to admit that the man had a point there.

''I'll grant you that,'' Clint finally said, ''but I'm here to make sure you know, Thorpe, that I don't like it.''

He turned on his heels and walked towards the door, then turned to face the somewhat indecisive lawman.

''Just make sure you tell McCoy that I'll be conducting my own little investigation, and if I find out that he sent those men—if I can prove it—I'll be coming for him, through you, through Bennett Ransom, and through anybody else he thinks he can send against me.''

TWENTY-SEVEN

Next stop was the blacksmith, who also doubled as a horse doctor. The smithy did not have his forge set up in the livery stable, but in a small lean-to of his own. The Gunsmith had to walk down an alley to reach the smithy, and it wasn't without some trepidation that he did so.

Clint found the man working over his forge and waited for him to pause before trying to get his attention.

There were several stalls in the lean-to, where horses that the smith would be working on would normally stand, although the stalls were empty at the moment. In one stall Clint thought he spotted something, and stepped inside for a closer look. By moving some hay and dirt around with his foot, he uncovered what looked like a large, dried bloodstain, but he had no way of knowing whether the blood had come from a horse or a man.

As Clint stepped out of the stall, the smithy looked up and saw him.

"Are you the blacksmith?" Clint asked.

The man stared at the Gunsmith as if he were crazy and said, "Yes, I am."

The smith was a tall, beefy man in his fifties, with steel gray hair, bulging biceps and a belly that was beginning to get soft.

"My name is Otto," the man said, and Clint detected an accent that betrayed the man's German heritage. "What can I do for you?"

"I understand that when Doc Palance is not around, you've been known to do some doctoring."

The man shook his head and said, "On horses and some other animals."

"Not people?"

The man shook his granite block-shaped head.

"No one has come to you for treatment of a gunshot wound since last night?"

"No."

Clint took out some folding money and showed it to the big smith. "I'd pay for the information, Otto."

"There is no information to pay for," the man said, eyeing the money.

Clint decided to try a different tactic, although he kept the money in his hand, in plain sight.

"There's a lot of blood on the floor of this stall here," Clint said.

"So?"

"Looks like somebody tried to cover it up too," Clint added. He stepped into the stall and bent to examine the stain closer. He felt the big smith's presence behind him as he touched his hand to the ground.

"Still damp," he said.

He turned and looked at the big German, who stared right back at him. It was odd to him that the man was not trying to explain away the stain. Maybe it wasn't in the man to lie, and the less he said, the less he was bothered by the situation.

I wonder, Clint thought, standing up, *whether Ransom paid the big blacksmith to be quiet . . . or threatened him?*

The blacksmith backed up to allow the Gunsmith to get out of the stall, then just stood there, solid as a rock, waiting for the next question.

"I get the feeling," Clint said, "that you'd like to tell me what I want to know, but you can't. I get the feeling you're an honest man, Otto, and that lying hurts you."

The man stared stolidly at Clint, without a flicker of emotion on his face.

"I'd say that a man named Bennett Ransom was here with a wounded man, and told you to take care of him and keep your mouth shut," Clint said, looking closely for a flicker of something in the man's face to satisfy him.

"All right, Otto," Clint said, putting his money away. *Sure,* he thought, he could have tried threatening the man, but it wasn't in the Gunsmith to do that to what he thought was a proud man. "I'll leave you to your work."

The man turned then and walked back to his forge, and Clint turned to leave.

"Mister," the man called.

"Yes?" Clint said, turning back.

"I would appreciate it if you would leave some of that money behind," Otto said.

Clint frowned and asked, "Why is that?"

"Things have been very slow," Otto said, getting

ready to turn his attention to his forge. "I have not been called upon to treat a wounded animal for some time now."

Clint stared at the man, but Otto was already back at his forge. The Gunsmith took some money out of his pocket, set it down on a nearby wooden bench, and then turned and left, satisfied.

Clint met Terry Battles back at the hotel, and together they walked to the livery to pick up the buckboard and Duke.

"What did you find out?" she asked on the way.

"The blacksmith, a big German named Otto, did treat someone today," he answered, "and it was someone who was doing a whole lot of bleeding."

"Who was it?"

"That I didn't find out," he said, "but whoever it was, I'd bet my last dollar that he's dead. Nobody could lose that much blood and stay around to talk about it."

"Good," she said. "I'm glad he's dead."

He looked at her quickly and said, "The dead man's not the one who shot your brother. I'd bet my next to last dollar that was Bennett Ransom."

"Then he should be killed next," she said, viciously.

"You're a little bloodthirsty today, aren't you?" Clint asked her.

She looked back at him, then looking ashamed said, "Yeah, maybe I am . . . and I don't much like it."

"Well, cheer up then," he said. "Tim's going to be fine, and it'll be some time before McCoy, Ransom and their men try another nighttime attack like last night."

"Maybe you're right," she said, "but what will they try next?"

"If I knew that," he told her, "I'd take my own advice and cheer up."

TWENTY-EIGHT

The trip back up the mountain went much the way the trip down had. They made the back of the buckboard as comfortable as they could for Tim Battles, and Terry sat back there with him.

"Damn, but this bandage is tight," Tim complained.

"The doctor made it that way on purpose, Tim," Terry told him. "He doesn't want your shoulder to start bleeding again during the trip up."

"Well, just as long as we can loosen it up some when we get back," he grumbled.

"We'll see," Terry said as if she were speaking to a little boy who had just asked if he could have a piece of candy.

"I hope everything is all right up there," Tim said.

"Relax, Tim," she said. "Tod can handle things just fine without us."

"For a while, maybe," Tim said.

"We haven't even been gone a full day, Tim," Terry argued.

"It seems a lot longer," he complained.

"You know, if you're gonna constantly be complaining I'm gonna tell Clint to turn this buckboard around and take you right back to town."

"And I'll do it too," Clint said, speaking for the first time. Up until that point, he had been satisfied to let brother and sister converse without interfering.

"All right, all right," Tim said sourly. "Stop ganging up on me."

"Just relax, Tim," she said. "You're supposed to be resting, remember?"

"Yeah, yeah."

Clint turned around and Terry caught his eye and shook her head. This wasn't going to be easy, her look said. He nodded his agreement, then turned and directed his attention to missing most of the bumps.

"Tim!" Tod Battles called out when he saw the buckboard bearing his brother. Immediately, the wagon was surrounded by well-wishers, all clamoring to hear how Battles was.

"Let's get him inside," Clint told Tod, while Terry was kept busy fielding questions.

"We lost half of our hut," Tod told Clint. "We closed off what was left of it so that Terry could use it herself, and we've blocked off a small section in the bunkhouse for Tim. We figured he'd need some room."

"That's going to make it real close in there," Clint remarked.

"The men don't mind," Tod said. "Most of these guys would do anything Tim asked them to do."

They moved around to the back of the buckboard to

ease Tim out, and the older brother immediately began bombarding Tod with questions.

"Work is going fine, Tim," Tod assured him. "Let us get you inside and then we can talk."

They got Tim settled into a bunk that had been sectioned off from the rest of the bunkhouse, and Clint left the two brothers to their discussion. Outside, he saw Terry breaking away from the crowd of men and heading for the bunkhouse.

"You came out of that unscathed?" Clint kidded her.

She grinned and said, "They were all so concerned about Tim. It's nice to see."

"I'm impressed with the regard his men have for your brother," Clint said.

"He treats them right," she said. "Oh, he gets mean sometimes—even with me and Tod—but only when he has to. Is he all right?"

"He's inside with Tod, getting an update."

"He's supposed to be resting."

"You go in and tell him."

"Oh, no," she said, shaking her head, "no women allowed in there. Besides, the smell would kill me."

Clint had to agree. A woman would not be able to put up with the gamy smell that sometimes pervaded a men's bunkhouse.

"Why don't you take a look at your own quarters, then?" Clint said. "Tod said they managed to save half of it for you."

"Come with me?" she invited.

"My pleasure," he said.

They walked through the camp to what had once been home for all three of the Battleses, and was now nothing more than a shack.

"I've seen outhouses that have looked bigger than that," she commented.

"Look at the bright side," he said.

"Where?" she asked. "It hardly looks like it has four sides, let alone a bright one."

"You'll have privacy," he said. "I'll bet you haven't had that in a long time."

"No," she said, with a speculative look on her face, "you're right about that. There could be some definite advantages to that, couldn't there, Clint?"

He looked closely at her then, walking beside him, and wondered if he were reading her tone correctly.

When they walked inside and shut the door behind them, he discovered that he was.

She turned swiftly into his arms and reached hungrily for his embrace, tongue darting avidly against his, hands working on his body. She was rapidly drawing him to a fever pitch, and although this may have been a viable place, it certainly was not the right time.

"Terry," he said when her mouth slid from him.

"I know," she said, resting her forehead against his chest, catching her breath. "I don't think I've ever attacked a man like that before."

"I'm honored to be the first," he said, and they both began to laugh.

"You had better look this place over," he suggested. "I'm sure Tod went to a lot of trouble to make it as comfortable as possible."

"Yes, you're right," she said, gently disengaging herself from his arms. "But later . . ." she said.

"Terry—"

"Tonight, Clint," she said, "when the others are asleep . . . please?"

He looked into her eyes and found himself saying,

"Yes, Terry, all right. Tonight."

"Good," she said, smiling happily, and then turning said, "Now let's see what we have here."

TWENTY-NINE

After Terry brought Tim his dinner in the bunk-house, she joined the others in the mess hall.

"We've been waiting for you," Tod said.

"Want to fill me in on what happened while we were gone?" she asked.

"Clint's been filling me in on what happened in town," Tod said. "Sounds like both sides lost a man last night."

Terry frowned and asked, "Who did we lose?"

"O'Toole."

"Damn," she snapped. "I didn't know."

"I'm sorry," Clint said, "I should have told you, but—"

"That's all right," she said, touching his arm. It was a move that did not escape the notice of Tod Battles. "We had other things on our minds."

She looked at Tod then, saw the way he was studying her and Clint, and she said, "Tim. We were worried about Tim."

"Oh," Tod said, and turned his attention back to his food.

"Things moving along here, Tod?" she asked.

"Sure," he said. "Chute's fixed, work's back underway—"

"On time?" she asked.

Tod gave his sister a look and a shrug.

"You tell Tim?" she asked.

"Oh, yeah."

"And?" she asked, impatiently.

"And I made a suggestion."

She stared at her younger brother for a few long seconds and then asked, "Highballin'?"

Tod nodded and said, "Tim agrees."

Terry looked annoyed and Clint said, "Anyone want to let me in on this? What exactly does highballing mean?"

"Means throwin' caution to the wind," she said. "It means losing more men than we have to on this operation . . ."

Tod looked at Clint and said, "It means working a little faster, is all."

"That *isn't* all," Terry insisted. "When you highball it things start to happen that shouldn't."

"Why?" Tod asked. "Things ain't been happenin' around here lately?"

"You know very well what I mean," Terry hissed, and stormed out of the mess.

"What's eating her?" Clint asked.

"Our pa was killed highballin' an operation," Tod said. "She's been afraid of it ever since."

"What about you and Tim?"

"Tim's done it before," Tod said. "He worked with Pa."

"How dangerous is it?"

Tod shrugged, said, "This work is always dangerous, so when you try to do it a little fast, it gets a little harder. Can't be helped, Clint. We ain't about to lose this mountain, not to the likes of McCoy.''

"It's your decision," Clint said. "Yours, Tim's . . . and Terry's. I'm just along for the ride.''

"The full ride?" Tod asked.

"Until I can think of something better to do," Clint said. *Or*, he added to himself, *until Ransom Bennett and McCoy are off your backs*.

Clint liked these people. They were hardworking, willing to bust their backs and risk their lives to make a living. People like Bennett and McCoy had no business trying to horn in and make it even harder on them.

"What about your men?" Clint asked. "Will they go along with it?"

"That's up to them," Tod said, "but when they hear it from Tim, they'll go along with it—most of them, anyway."

"Your brother commands a lot of respect," Clint said.

"Yeah," Tod said, "like my pa used to. Pa was a strong man, and Tim's the same way."

"Seems to me you're a lot like them," Clint said.

Tod looked pleased. "I hope so. God knows I'm trying."

"And succeeding, from what I can see," Clint said. "You seem to have done a fine job of cleaning up after last night."

"Wasn't much," Tod said, modestly. "Rebuilding the hut for Terry, burying O'Toole—''

"And keeping everyone's mind on work," Clint said. "That takes a leader, Tod."

"Tim's the leader," Tod said. "I'm just trying to follow in his footsteps."

"Well," Clint said, standing up from the table,

"that's all well and good, Tod, but there comes a time in a man's life when he's got to start making some footsteps of his own. I'm not saying that now's the time," he added, before Tod could speak, "I'm just saying it's something to think about."

The amount of room that had been cleared out in the bunkhouse for Big Tim Battles would normally have accommodated about ten men, so even though the logging crew was not up to full capacity, the bunkhouse was now very crowded. It was so crowded, in fact, that rather than add another body to the crush, the Gunsmith volunteered to sleep outside, which was really nothing new to him—and much preferred, considering the scent that pervaded the overcrowded bunkhouse.

Before turning in for the night, Clint found himself off to one side with Tod. They had set up the sentry schedule, with two on duty at a time. All of the men being used as sentries were volunteers this time, some of whom knew how to handle a gun, others of whom were instructed by the Gunsmith in how to use them.

"Do you really think they won't try again what they tried last night?" Tod asked.

"Even if they were going to think twice after last night," Clint said, "they'll think still again when they see two armed sentries."

"I hope so," Tod said. "I wish you'd let me take one of the guard spots myself, though."

"I think your men realize that you need to be well rested to run this operation," Clint said, "especially with your brother laid up. Besides, I'll be taking one of the final spots myself."

"We really appreciate this, Clint," Tod said.

"Don't forget," Clint told him, "I'm on the payroll, remember?"

"And at a bargain too," Tod said. He patted the Gunsmith on the back and said, "Good night, then. I'll see you in the morning—and not before, I hope."

"Good night, Tod," Clint said.

Tod went into the bunkhouse, and Clint found a clearing where he spread out his bedroll. He had barely done so when he became aware of someone behind him. He turned and found Terry Battles watching him.

"Terry," he said, "you shouldn't be out here."

"Why not?" she asked. "I own part of this mountain, don't I?"

"That you do," he agreed, "but in case something happens—"

"You said you didn't think anything would happen for a while," she reminded him.

"I know that—"

"Besides, I didn't do too badly last night, did I?" she went on.

"No, you didn't."

"Besides, I came out here for a good reason."

"That being?"

"You," she said, and her meaning was plain to see in her eyes.

"Terry—"

"I want you, Clint," she said, "and I think you want me. There's no reason why we shouldn't—"

"I could think of a couple," he interrupted.

"My brothers?"

"For starters."

"My brothers don't run my life, Clint," she said. "We're business partners up here."

"And family."

"That may be," she said, "but that don't give them the right to run my life."

"Terry," he argued, "up here it wouldn't be much of a secret for long—"

"I don't want it to be," she said, grabbing him by the arm, "and I don't expect any promises beyond tonight, or next week, if that's what you're worried about."

"I'm not worried," he said.

"Then what is it?" she asked. "Are you afraid that maybe you'll fall in love with me?"

"That's not impossible," he said, "although I'm not worried about it."

"Then come with me," she said, pulling on his arm. "Come to my bed, Clint Adams."

There was no denying the fact that he wanted her, and since they were both adults, and the only alternative was sleeping on the ground, he said, "All right, Terry. All right."

As they entered her hut together, Clint couldn't help hoping that they had done so unnoticed, for Terry's sake and for the sake of her brothers. He didn't know how they would feel about him and Terry, and he had come to think of them as friends. But Terry was also his friend, and what they were doing together they were doing as friends—closer than most, but still friends.

THIRTY

While they lay in each other's arms Terry said, "When I'm with you, I believe we'll beat McCoy, make our payments on time, and come out of this all right."

"I'm glad I instill so much confidence in you," he said, tightening his arms around her.

She began to kiss his chest, then his neck and finally worked her way up to his mouth. Their mouths worked hungrily, as if they were trying to devour each other, and she reached between them to take hold of his massive erection.

"God, I want you so much . . ." she breathed into his mouth. She moved one warm, silken thigh over him, then slid her body atop his. She rubbed her pubic thatch against his cock, then pushed harder, stroking and inflaming him.

Clint reached down to take hold of her hips, then lifted her up and impaled her on his pulsating rod.

"Oh, yes," she said, settling down on him, enjoying the way he filled her. She flattened her hands against his chest and began to rotate on him, seeking new sensations, moving her hips this way and that and moaning aloud. Once she was so loud that Clint hoped the guards outside wouldn't hear her.

"I'm going to have to find some way to keep you quieter," he said to her.

She opened her eyes and looked down at him and he noticed that they seemed slightly out of focus. She smiled at him and touched his face.

"Even if someone hears me, maybe they'll think I'm having a bad dream," she said. She laughed again and added, "That couldn't be further from the truth, could it?"

"No," he said, "but I'm still going to find a way to keep you quiet."

He moved quickly, turning over so that his cock popped free of her. He put her on her back and then even before his tool, slick with her love juices, could cool from the draft, he plunged it into her wet sheath again. As she opened her mouth to gasp or moan, he covered it with his, so that whatever sound she made she made into his mouth.

His hips worked convulsively now, with a life of their own, increasing speed until finally she began to writhe beneath him and he began to spurt inside of her. When her body relaxed beneath his he moved his mouth from hers and they both gasped for breath.

"What were you trying to do," she asked, "suffocate me?"

"Keep you quiet, is all," he said.

She kissed him shortly then and said, "I heartily approve of your method, sir."

"I'm glad," he said, "because I plan to use it very often."

"I look forward to it," she replied. "Can I look forward to the next time being very soon?"

Since they both knew that he was showing no signs of shriveling inside of her, they both knew the answer to that question.

"I'm ready when you are," he said.

She grinned and said, "Oh, I'm ready."

When Clint rose to leave, Terry argued.

"It's still early," she said.

"I have the last watch of the night," he told her, "and I don't want anyone to have to go looking for their relief."

"Why not?" she asked. "I had to go looking for mine, didn't I?"

THIRTY-ONE

The next week was relatively uneventful—except for the three injuries that resulted from the highballing. Luckily, none of the accidents was fatal, but Terry felt they were avoidable, and argued with Tod.

"Don't argue with me," Tod said, "argue with your other brother. He's the bull of the woods, not me."

"He's in no shape to argue," she said.

"You must be kidding," Tod said. "That's all he's been doing since he came back."

"Well, we shouldn't be letting him," she said vehemently.

"How do you propose we stop him?" Tod asked. "Maybe we should have left him back in town."

Clint, who was sitting next to them at chow, leaned over and said, "That would have been a good way to get him killed."

They both stared at him.

"Just because McCoy's been quiet for a week doesn't mean you're not still in a fight," he told them.

"I thought maybe . . ." Terry said, letting it trail off.

"Maybe what? That he'd given up?" Clint asked.

132

"Men like McCoy don't give up that easily."

"But one of his men was killed," she pointed out.

"That's a small price for a man like him to pay for what he wants," Clint said.

"Why do you think he's waiting?" Tod asked.

"He's trying to lull you into a false sense of security," Clint said. "He's trying to make you think just the way you're thinking now, about work and not about him."

"And that's when he strikes?"

"Right."

Tod and Terry exchanged glances, and then Terry said, "I guess we're lucky to have Clint around, to keep reminding us."

"Yeah," Tod said, looking first at Clint and then at his sister, "among other reasons."

Clint looked at Tod, but the younger man averted his face quickly, and it was impossible to read his expression. Did he know that Clint had been spending almost every night in the hut with Terry?

Did anybody not know it?

"What are we waiting for?" Bennett Ransom said. "That's what I want to know."

McCoy looked at Ransom and said, "We are waiting for me to give the go-ahead."

"Then what are *you* waiting for?"

McCoy looked at Ransom again, this time longer, but the man simply returned his glare.

"I am not used to having my employees question my actions, Ransom," he said.

The relationship between McCoy and Ransom had been changing subtly for weeks, and now suddenly the metamorphosis was almost complete.

Bennett Ransom sat down.

"Wha—" McCoy began, but Ransom did not give him a chance to protest.

"There's one thing we'd better make clear right now, McCoy," Ransom said. "I am not your employee, I am your partner."

"You're mad," McCoy said. "Get out of my chair."

"We can clear this matter up right now, McCoy," Ransom said.

"How?"

Ransom shrugged. "You want me out of this," he said, "you put me out."

McCoy closed his hands in tight fists of rage, but he did not move from behind his desk. The look in Bennett Ransom's eyes told the banker that if he moved, the gunman would kill him.

"That's it then, *Mr*. McCoy," Ransom said, crossing his legs. "We're partners."

McCoy pulled his chair out and sat down behind his desk, refusing to feel defeated. All right, let Ransom think they were partners for a while. McCoy was sure the man would still be controllable—perhaps even more so—because the banker was still the brains. Ransom still wouldn't move until McCoy gave the word, so nothing was really changed.

McCoy would just have to put up with Ransom's filthy presence in his office, and on his furniture.

Until the time came to kill him, that is.

Of course, McCoy had no way of knowing that Bennett Ransom's thoughts were running along the same general lines.

THIRTY-TWO

It was the first payroll day since the Gunsmith's arrival in Olympia, and Tod was going to the Olympia bank to collect the money.

"I'd better come along," Clint said.

"You think they'd be satisfied with hitting the payroll?" Tod asked.

"Hitting the payroll would be relatively easy for McCoy, since he is the bank," Clint pointed out, "but I doubt that he'd be satisfied with that. It would be small change compared to what he could realize by taking your mountain from you."

"Then what—"

"Stealing your payroll would simply be another way to slow you down. If you weren't able to pay your men, some of them might walk out on you."

"Not my men," Tod said.

"You lost a few that first day in the saloon," Clint reminded him. "Did you expect that?"

"No," Tod admitted.

"Then I'll come along," Clint said, and there was no further argument.

"How about other men?" Tod asked.

Clint thought about that for a moment, but then decided against it. If it came to gunplay, he didn't want to have to worry about being hit by a bullet from his own side.

"I think we can handle it, Tod," Clint said.

"I'll bring a gun."

"Fine," Clint said.

"I'm coming, too," Terry said. Up until that moment, she had been content to listen to the discussion.

"I don't think that's wise," Clint said.

"Why?" she asked, her temper flaring. "Is it because I'm a woman?"

"No, it's because you're a Battles," Clint said, "and the only one in any shape to stay up here in control."

"But—"

"If you come too," Clint said, trying a new tact, "you can be damn sure that Big Tim is going to get out of that bed. Do you want that?"

"No," she said, still seething although she knew that he was right.

"All right, then," he said. Clint turned to Tod and said, "Let's put some guards out all day, just to be on the safe side."

"Right," Tod said, and went off to take care of it.

"Do you think McCoy will make a move today?" Terry asked him.

"I think today would be a good day for it, yes," he answered. "I hope I'm wrong."

"Why?"

"Because," Clint explained, "if he tries to take this payroll today, somebody is going to get killed."

"Well," she said, touching his arm, "as long as it's

not Tod or you, I'd say he was bringing that on himself."

"Oh, make no mistake," Clint said, "McCoy won't be in any immediate danger. It'll be Bennett Ransom out there with the lead flying, not McCoy."

"Ransom is dangerous, isn't he?" she asked.

"Anyone with a gun in his hand is dangerous," Clint said, "but Bennett Ransom with a gun in his hand is lethal."

"But so are you," she said.

"Yeah," he said, looking over her shoulder at Tod, who was coming back, "there is that."

They saddled a horse for Tod. Clint decided against taking the wagon to town for the payroll. The money could be carried in their saddlebags just as easily.

"If we have to move fast," he explained to Terry and Tod, "the wagon will only slow us down."

"All right," Tod said. "You know best about this sort of thing, Clint."

"Let's hope so," Clint said.

They mounted up and Terry told them, "Be careful, both of you. Come back safe."

Tod Battles looked down at his sister and grinned. It was a mischievous grin that made him look even younger than his nineteen years.

"Don't worry, sis," he said. "I'll bring him back to you in one piece."

She stared at her brother and said, "What are you talking about? I want you both back."

Tod laughed and wheeled his horse around. Terry looked at Clint who winked at her, turned Duke and followed Tod down the mountain.

THIRTY-THREE

When Clint Adams and Tod Battles rode into town, they knew that there was at least one set of eyes on them that were owned by McCoy.

"I just thought of something that gives me the chills," Tod said.

"What?"

"What if McCoy don't turn our payroll money over to us?" Tod asked.

"He won't do that."

"Why not?"

"If he does he might as well close his bank," Clint explained. "That's his legitimate business, and he's got to run it honestly. No, if he's going to try and keep the payroll from getting up the hill, he'll have someone try and take it from us along the way."

"Ransom?"

"Who else?"

"You can take him, can't you, Clint?"

"We'll have to wait and see, won't we?" Clint said.

"Do you think it will come to that?"

"I know it will," Clint said shortly. "I've known it

since the beginning . . . and there isn't a thing I can do about it.''

''You could leave town.''

Clint smiled bitterly and said, ''I've got enough young bucks gunning for my rep as it is. If I run away from one, there'll just be that many more after me. No, Tod, I can't leave town. If I do, I'd never be able to enter another one.''

''I understand,'' Tod said. ''I guess having a reputation like yours isn't what I always thought it would be.''

''I guess not,'' Clint said. ''I'm sorry to disappoint you.''

One man who wasn't disappointed was Bennett Ransom. When he was told that Clint Adams and the kid were in town, he knew things were going according to plan.

''They're here for the payroll,'' Ransom said to Deacon Platt, the bearer of the news.

''Should I go tell Mr. McCoy?'' Platt asked.

Ransom took the long, thin cigar he was smoking out of his mouth and said, ''What for? They're headed for the bank, ain't they? He'll know soon enough.''

''What should I do, then?''

''Just get the boys together, Deke,'' Ransom said, ''and wait for me.''

''What does Mr. McCoy want us to—''

Ransom jabbed Platt in the chest with a stiff forefinger and said, ''Forget about McCoy, Platt. You do what I tell you from now on, you got that?''

Platt was about to question Ransom further, but when he looked into the gunman's eyes he simply nodded and said, "I got you, Ransom."

"Good," Ransom said. "Now go do what you were told."

"Right."

Ransom watched as Deacon Platt left his hotel room, and then the gunman walked to the window to look out at the street. He looked at the cigar in his hand, then placed it in his mouth and drew deeply on it. By the time the cigar was finished, Adams and the kid should be ready to go back up the mountain with the payroll. Ransom recalled a time when he would have been satisfied to kill them, take the money and run, but he had bigger fish to fry now. The payroll was only a small part of it . . . but Clint Adams, now *he* was a big part. Once he killed the Gunsmith, McCoy would be his for the taking. Ransom figured that he'd not only have the mountain, but the bank too.

Yes sir, very shortly, Ransom would have everything he ever wanted, and when he did—well, then he'd just go looking for more.

Clint and Tod stopped their horses in front of the bank and dismounted. Tod removed his saddlebags from his horse and carried them inside with him.

"Afternoon, Mr. Battles," the teller greeted.

"I'm here for our payroll," Tod said. Clint remained quiet and let Tod handle the transaction.

"Of course, sir. Just step over to our manager's desk, please."

Tod took the saddlebags off the teller's window and carried them to the manager's desk, where the slight, bespectacled man sat. He was alternating nervous glances between Clint Adams and McCoy's office door.

"My payroll," Tod said, dropping his saddlebags on the man's desk.

"Yes, Mr. Battles," the man said. "Of course."

The manager got up, went to the safe which had already been opened, and removed the stacks of money that made up the Battleses' payroll. He cast another nervous glance at McCoy's door, then carried the money to his desk.

"You'll have to sign for it, of course," he said to Tod.

"Of course," Tod said.

The manager extended a sheet of paper towards him and Tod took it, read it through, and signed it. It was simply a receipt for the money, signifying that the payroll had been picked up by an authorized member of the Battles camp.

"Thank you very much," Tod said, filling his saddlebags equally with the money. "I appreciate it."

"Not at all," the man replied. He threw one last wary glance at Clint, and then looked down at his desk.

"Let's go," Tod told Clint, slinging the saddlebags over his shoulder.

Clint followed Tod out of the bank, alert even though he doubted that Ransom would make a move while they were still in town.

When they mounted up Tod said, "Well, back up the mountain, huh?"

"No," Clint said.

"No? Why not?" Tod asked, confused.

"Let's make one stop first."

"Where?"

"The saloon."

"What for?" Tod demanded, more confused than ever. Why would Clint want to stop at the saloon when they were carrying so much money?

"We've got to go up the mountain, don't we?" Clint asked.

"Well, sure, but—"

"Well," Clint said, wheeling Duke around and heading him in the direction of the saloon, "mountain climbing is thirsty work."

When Ransom saw Clint and Tod come out of the bank he stubbed out the butt of his cigar and strapped on his gun. Picking up his hat he was preparing to walk from the window and leave his room when he stopped short.

"What the—" he said.

Adams was turning his horse and heading not towards the mountain, but away from it. What the hell was he doing? Ransom watched intently as Tod urged his horse to follow Clint, and watched as the two men rode to the saloon, dismounted and went in.

"They must be drunk already," he said to himself. Why else would they be going into the saloon while carrying all that money?

Better and better, he thought. Sure, he had the Gunsmith scared, that was it. Why else would the man need a drink at a time like this?

This would make it even easier, he thought. He put his hat down on the table next to him, leaned the heel of his right hand on the butt of his gun, and settled down to wait just a little longer.

Hell, he'd waited this long, what harm would a few more minutes be?

They were in the saloon long enough to have one drink each, and when they came out the saddlebags were still over Tod Battles's shoulder. They mounted up and this time they headed out of town towards the mountain, with Clint Adams in the lead.

Thinking, *At last!* Bennett Ransom picked up his hat and left his hotel room.

For years Clint had been aware of his sixth sense, whether it be real or imagined. Some people would have called it an old lawman's instinct, others might have called it a gunman's instinct. Whatever it was called, it had worked for him many times in the past, saving his life by keeping him alive when a "normal" man might have died.

As they rode up the mountain back to the camp, Clint was counting on that extra sense of his to be working overtime.

This time it had to keep two men alive.

THIRTY-FOUR

"My back itches," Tod said.

"That's good," Clint said. "It means that you're alert and aware."

"It also means I could be dead in a matter of seconds," Tod replied.

"That's true."

Tod, aware that he was sweating heavily beneath his coat, looked at Clint and asked, "How can you be so calm?"

"Comes with practice," Clint said. "I realized a long time ago that to lose my head meant losing my life. That's something I'd like to avoid as long as possible."

"Me too," Tod said, with feeling.

"Now let's ride the rest of the way in silence, all right?" Clint suggested.

"Do you think you'll be able to hear them coming?"

"Tod," Clint said, "I'm hoping that I'll *feel* them coming long before they make a move."

Farther on up the slope Deacon Platt and five other

men were waiting impatiently for Bennett Ransom to show up.

"I hope he shows up before they do," one of the other men said.

"Well, if he doesn't," Platt said, "we'll just have to take them, that's all."

"What's wrong with Ransom, anyway?" the other man asked. "I think he's gone crazy or something."

"Yeah," Platt said. "You tell *him* that."

"Not me," the man said. "I'm not about to go up against his gun."

"Neither am I," Platt said. "Listen, if Ransom can take over from McCoy I'll go with him, otherwise I'll stay with McCoy."

"I'll stay where the money is, Deke."

"And so will I."

"Do you think Ransom will be able to take the Gunsmith?" the other man asked.

"I don't know, Joe," Platt said. "I've seen Ransom's move, and I've never seen a faster one."

"Well, I haven't seen the Gunsmith's move," Joe Earle said, "but I did see him in that saloon the first day, ready to take on six men. He's a cool one. If he's half as fast as his reputation says he is—"

"Would you be willing to make a bet?" Platt asked.

Earle studied Platt for a second, then said, "You mean you want to bet me that Ransom can take Adams? How much are we talking about?"

"Well, we're all gonna make a bundle here, ain't we?" Platt asked. "How about one-third?"

"A third of my share against a third of yours?"

"Sure, why not. Makes it interesting."

"And I've got the Gunsmith?"

"That's who you want, ain't it?"

"Well, sure—but wait a minute."

"What's the matter?" Platt asked.

Looking confused, Joe Earle, who was only a couple of years older than Platt, said, "Ain't we waiting here to kill Adams?"

"Yeah."

Earle frowned at Platt now and said, "And if we do kill him, he can't outdraw Ransom and I lose the bet."

"I didn't think of that," Platt said with a sly look.

"I'll bet you didn't," Earle said.

"Hey, if this Gunsmith is so good, do you really think we're gonna be able to kill him?"

"You talk fast, Platt," Earle said. "If I didn't know better I'd think you was trying to con me out of a third of my share."

"All right, all right," Platt said. "If the Gunsmith comes out of this alive, the bet's on. All right?"

Earle thought that over for a moment, then nodded and said, "All right."

"Shh," Platt said then. "I hear someone coming." He waved to the other three men to be ready, and then put his hand on his gun and waited. He hoped it was Ransom, but if it wasn't, he was ready for that too.

It was too bad they had to kill Adams. He'd been looking forward to seeing him face Ransom ever since the man had come to town.

Maybe they'd be able to take that payroll without killing him.

That thought was Deacon Platt's mistake. He should have been hoping that they'd be able to take the payroll without getting killed.

●　　●　　●

Bennett Ransom's horse had the misfortune to step on a stone and raise a serious bruise soon after they left town.

"Stupid animal," Ransom said, dropping the horse's bruised hoof to the ground.

He had intended to take a shorter route up the slope to reach the point where his men were waiting. Now he'd have to go on foot, and that would mean he was going to miss the action.

Now he wished he had sent more than six men. Facing the Gunsmith, they were going to be in trouble without him.

Serious trouble.

"Stop," Clint said.

"What's wrong?" Tod asked.

"The path we're following narrows up ahead, doesn't it?" Clint asked.

"Yeah, I think so." Tod looked at Clint quickly and asked, "Do you think that's where—"

"It's a good spot for it," Clint said. He hesitated a moment, studying the surrounding area, then said, "Wait here," and started Duke forward.

"Wait a minute," Tod said, holding out his hand. "Where are you going?"

"Up ahead a ways."

"I can't let you do that, Clint," Tod said. "Not alone."

"Tod," Clint said, "when the lead starts flying I don't want to have to worry about you. You make a pretty big target, you know."

"Yeah, but—"

"Besides," Clint explained further, "this is what

you're paying me for.''

"Sure," Tod said, "a dollar. That don't seem worth the risk you're taking."

"When we're finished here," Clint said, "we'll talk about a raise. Wait here," he added, and started forward.

THIRTY-FIVE

Clint knew he could play it two ways. He could get off his horse and approach on foot, silently, or he could give Duke a good kick in the sides and charge ahead at full speed. He decided to take it on the run, which he hoped would throw the waiting men off balance.

"All right, big boy," he told Duke, "make yourself as skinny as possible, it's going to start raining lead."

Duke shook his massive head back and forth to convey his displeasure, but Clint knew that the big black gelding would perform flawlessly, as he always did.

Clint leaned over and whispered in Duke's ear, "Go," and the gelding was off like a shot.

"Holy shit!" Joe Earle said. Clint Adams was coming right at them, riding his big black horse at full speed. Earle didn't know about the others, but he wasn't quite prepared for that sight.

"What do we do?" he yelled out.

Platt, also thrown off balance, yelled, "Shoot," and fired wildly.

The single shot was all the Gunsmith needed to tell him where the ambushers were.

When the first shot came Bennett Ransom lifted his head and listened for the second, but he couldn't hear it. There were too many shots for him to pick out the second one.

Shaking his head he listened to the sound of the shots, and knew that they were being fired in panic.

"Idiots," he said, abandoning his horse—which he had been leading—and breaking into a run.

Coolness under fire, Clint thought. It made a good soldier, and he had seen it make a lot of men walk away from a gunfight with faster men. It didn't matter how fast you got your gun out if you didn't hit anything once you started firing.

As soon as he heard the first shot he drew his gun, located the source, and calmly began to return the fire. Still, even the worst marksman can hit something accidentally, so as soon as he had them spotted he dismounted and sent Duke on, out of danger, making sure he had his Springfield with him.

Finding cover, he holstered his gun and coolly continued to fire with his rifle.

The first five shots fired by the Gunsmith killed two men, and the others fired back in blind panic.

"He's crazy," Joe Earle said.

"We'd better get out of here," Deacon Platt said, "while we still can."

As they started to retreat to their horses, Earle grabbed Platt's arm and asked, "Is the bet on?"

Platt paused a moment, then said, "All right, the bet's on—as long as we get away from here alive!"

"Jesus," Tod Battles said as he rode up on the scene. He saw the two men Clint was bent over and asked, "Are they dead?"

"They're dead," Clint said. He stood up, removed his gun from his holster, ejected the empty shells, reloaded and replaced the weapon.

"All that shooting," Tod said. "I was sure you were dead."

"Trying to save a dollar, Tod?" Clint asked.

Tod opened his mouth to answer, taking the question half seriously, but Clint cut him off.

"Never mind," he said, mounting Duke. "Ransom wasn't here. I don't know why, but he can't be far off. Let's get going. I've killed enough men for one day."

When Ransom came on the scene he stopped and put his hands on his hips. *This should have worked, damn it,* he thought, and two of his men were lying there dead.

"Damn it," he said aloud. Damn his horse for stepping on a stone, and damn Platt, Earle and the others for botching the job without him—although he had fully expected them to do so. They just weren't equipped to deal with a man like Clint Adams.

He was, though. This just proved that he was going to have to take care of Clint Adams—the Gunsmith—himself, face to face, once and for all, before the Battleses could be properly dealt with.

Casting a disgusted look at the dead men, he turned and began walking back to where he'd left his horse, formulating in his mind the explanation he was going to give McCoy for their failure to get the payroll. McCoy would undoubtedly come up with another idea, because he *was* the idea man, but his plan would have to wait.

The next order of business was the death of the Gunsmith.

THIRTY-SIX

"You made it," Terry called out as Clint and Tod rode into camp.

"I told you I'd bring him back in one piece," Tod said, casting a sideways glance at Clint.

"Did you have any trouble?" she asked.

"None to speak of," Clint said, before Tod could answer.

They both dismounted and one of the men took their horses. Tod slid his saddlebags off his horse as it was being led away.

"Is that it?" she asked.

"Uh, Terry—" Tod began.

"Let me have it," she said. "The men want their money."

She took the saddlebags from her brother and started towards the mess hall, where she would dispense the payroll. Tod followed, trying to get her attention, and Clint came after, maintaining his silence. This was, after all, a family matter.

Inside the mess hall Terry put the saddlebags down on a table and started undoing the straps.

"Terry, before you open that I should tell you—"

Terry opened one saddlebag and took the newspaper that was inside.

"—that there's only newspaper inside," Tod finished.

She looked at Tod, then opened the other saddlebag and took the newspaper out of that one too.

Staring at her brother she said, "There's only newspaper in these saddlebags."

"That's what I said."

She looked at Clint and said, "You've been awful quiet. Would you like to tell me why there is newspaper in these saddlebags? Maybe I'll believe it coming from you."

"Ter—"

"We left the money at the saloon," Clint said.

Terry's jaw dropped and she looked accusingly at her little brother.

"Poker?" she demanded. "You played poker with our payroll money?"

"You know me better than that, Terry," Tod said.

Terry paused a moment, then turned to Clint and started to say, "You played—"

"It wasn't me," Clint said.

"Then who played—"

"Easy, Terry," Clint said. "The money's on the way."

"On the way where?" she demanded. "You know, Tim is gonna have a fit if he finds out you lost that money."

"Terry, would I lose your payroll?" Clint asked innocently.

"I didn't think so," she said, "but now I'm not so

sure." She pointed to the newspaper and said, "Where is it?"

"I told you, it's on the way," Clint said. "It ought to be here within the hour."

"Are you sure?"

"Look," Clint said by way of explanation, "just remember, a dollar of that money is mine. When it comes to my own money, I don't fool around."

THIRTY-SEVEN

It was less than an hour later when a young blond woman on a line-back dun came riding into camp.

"Now who is she?" Terry asked aloud, but there was no one around to answer her.

As the woman rode towards the center of the compound Terry approached on foot and met her.

"Hello," the woman said, pulling her horse to a stop.

"Can I help you?" Terry asked, putting her hands on her hips.

The two women stayed that way for a few moments, looking each other over. Both finally decided that there was definitely something they didn't like about each other—and that was without knowing that they had both been in bed with the same man recently.

"Yes, I'm looking for Clint Adams."

"Really?" Terry asked. "Do you have some business with Mr. Adams?"

"Yes, as a matter of fact, I do," the woman replied. "Is he around?"

"I would have to check around," Terry said.

"That's all right," the other woman said, dismounting. When she hit the ground Terry noticed that she was shorter than herself, but that she had to admit that the woman had a more feminine figure. The sort of figure you saw in a saloon, wearing a sequined dress.

"I'll wait," the other said.

The two women faced each other for a few moments, and then Terry said, " 'Scuse me."

She found Clint in the bunkhouse talking to Tim, who was laughing uproariously when she entered.

"What the hell is going on here?" she demanded.

Both men looked at her and Tim said from his bed, "Terry, this man is a genius."

"I think I might like to argue that if I had the time," she commented. "That money still hasn't gotten here."

"It will," Big Tim assured her. "It will."

"Clint," she said, "there's someone here to see you."

"Who?" Clint asked, exchanging glances with Tim.

"A blond woman," Terry said, and the acid on her tongue was plain for both men to see. "She looks like a saloon girl."

"That's probably because that's just what she is," Clint said, getting to his feet. "I guess I'd better go out and see her before some of the men get a hold of her."

"The way she looks," Terry said, "she might enjoy that."

"Terry—" Tim said, warningly.

"You might as well come with me, Terry," Clint said. "You might find that she has something that will interest you."

Terry laughed and said, "That woman couldn't possibly have anything that would interest me." Her curiosity, however, compelled her to follow Clint out to the compound.

"Candace," she heard him say. "Hi."

"I'm here," the woman said, a statement Terry considered very dumb. Everyone could see that she was there.

"And do you have it?" Clint asked.

"Of course I have it," Candace answered. "You gave it to me, didn't you?"

"Yes, I did."

Candace removed her saddlebags from her horse and handed them to Clint.

"Did you think I was going to run with it?" she asked.

"The thought had never crossed my mind," Clint said. He turned and, handing the saddlebags to Terry, said, "These are yours."

"Mine?" Terry asked, staring at them. "Those aren't mine."

"Maybe the bags aren't," Clint said, "but the money inside is."

"What?"

"This here's your payroll, ma'am," Clint said.

THIRTY-EIGHT

"I don't care what his reasons were," Terry said tightly to her brother, Tod. They were seated at one of the tables in the mess hall, doling out the payroll to the men, who were lined up inside and outside. "He had no right to give that woman our money."

"Believe me, Terry," Tod said, "I thought he was crazy when we got to the saloon and he told me what he had in mind, but it made sense. The possibility was there that we would be killed, and if that happened he didn't want Ransom to get the payroll."

"There should have been another way," she said.

Tod examined his sister critically, and then said, "I think you're upset for a totally different reason, Terry."

"Such as what?" she asked, handing one of the men his money.

"I think you're jealous."

She threw him a furious look that almost singed his eyebrows, and when the man at the table cleared his throat she looked at him and demanded, "What?"

He jumped back half a step and said, "I—I just want my money."

"Oh," she said.

"I'll give it to you, George," Tod said, and started counting it out.

Terry was furious now with Clint, Tod, the blonde and most of all with herself for being furious. Tod was right, she was jealous, and that was what made her the angriest.

She had no claim on Clint, she knew that, and he had made sure that payroll arrived all right, but she was still angry. Damn it, that was a woman's right, to be angry when she knew she had no right to be angry.

The next man stepped up to the table and she said to Tod, "I can count this one out."

When she looked up Clint said, "That won't take much. It's only a dollar."

"I really shouldn't be letting you," Terry said to Clint later that night.

"Why not?"

"I'm angry with you."

"Still?"

"Well," she said, then paused to catch her breath before continuing. "Well . . . I was."

"And now?"

"Ohh . . . n-now I'm n-not sure," she said, bringing her hips up off the bed.

"When . . . will you be . . . sure?" he asked, sliding his hands beneath her.

"Oh, God . . . I don't know . . . Damn you, stop talking and go faster . . ."

She wrapped her powerful legs around him and he said, "Glad to oblige."

He began to drive his engorged penis into her at an increased pace and soon the only sound in the room was that of their flesh slapping together, joined by an occasional moan of pleasure from Terry. Then as her orgasm approached she began to call to him aloud—as she always did—and he still wondered if she could be heard from outside by anyone. There were times during the day when he examined the faces of some of the men to see if he could tell, but he couldn't. If anyone heard, they were kind enough—or smart enough—not to mention it.

After her orgasm he did not decrease his tempo, and soon she was climbing the peak again, and this time they reached it together and went over, and as he emptied into her she drummed her heels against his buttocks.

"God," he said afterward, "I guess you are still mad, aren't you?"

"What makes you say that?" she asked, caressing his limp penis.

"My butt is gonna be bruised for weeks," he said. "I'm not going to be able to sit a horse for at least that long."

"I'm not so dumb, then," she said, stroking him so that he began to harden again. "That'll keep you around for at least that much longer."

"Who said you were dumb?"

"Nobody," she said, "but I'm not."

"Not if you keep doing what you're doing now, you're not," he assured her.

"Oh, you like this, huh?" she asked. He was large enough now for her to wrap her hand around him.

"If you keep it up, I may never leave," he said. Her hand was moving up and down steadily, now, and he lifted his hips to meet it. As soon as he said that he knew he shouldn't have, but what she was doing felt so good.

She knew he would leave soon, and she wanted to enjoy him as much as she could for as long as she could, so she said, "Liar," and lowered her head to begin using her mouth as well.

She wondered idly—and a bit angrily—if his saloon girl friend had done this for him.

McCoy sat behind his desk in his office at the bank, silently eyeing Bennett Ransom, whose filthy carcass was resting in one of his clean chairs.

"I still don't understand—" he started to say, but he was startled into silence when Ransom bounded out of his chair violently and slammed both hands down flat on his desk.

"Let's not go through that again, McCoy!" he snapped angrily. "My horse stepped on a stone and came up lame, all right? It could happen to anyone."

"Yes," McCoy stammered, "I—I guess it could."

"Look, I know what I've got to do," Ransom said, straightening up. "When you get some more bright ideas, you let me know, huh?"

Ransom hitched up his gunbelt, turned and stalked out of the office, leaving a shaken McCoy behind.

It was at that moment that McCoy began to formulate in his mind a telegram he would send the next day. Ransom was rapidly becoming as large a problem as Adams, and it was time to send for some help.

Some professional help.

THIRTY-NINE

For the next five days almost all of McCoy's attempts to harass and otherwise interfere with the Battles operation were stymied, thanks to Clint Adams's carefully placed lookouts. Once two loggers were injured when McCoy's men tried to bust their splash dam, but the attempt was unsuccessful. McCoy was becoming impatient, but he knew help was on the way.

Bennett Ransom did not know that help was on its way, but he too was becoming impatient. He could not storm the logging camp and call out the Gunsmith, and Adams had not yet come back into town following the payroll incident. He was forced to sit and wait, which was not his way of doing things. Because of this he was also becoming very irritable, and found it impossible to be around other people, especially McCoy. Communications had broken down between the two men, except for the odd occasion when Ransom chose to invade the banker's office and remind him that they were still partners.

That only served to increase McCoy's impatience.

● ● ●

Up on the mountain there was some impatience as well.

Big Tim was impatient to be back to work, but he was barely ready to get out of bed and start walking around.

Terry Battles was impatient with Tim, and Tod was impatient with McCoy and Ransom, waiting for their one big attempt at putting them out of business.

Clint Adams was impatient to be away. He'd stayed too long already, as evidenced by the increasing cold, and Terry's increasing possessiveness.

After five days on the mountain without a break, Clint was ready to go into town.

"What will you do if Ransom calls you out?" Tod asked as Clint saddled Duke.

"I'll cross that bridge when I come to it," Clint said. "I just need some time in town."

Tod was about to question him again, but from behind them another voice spoke.

"Let him go, Tod," Big Tim Battles said.

Both Clint and Tod turned to face the bull of the woods and Clint said, "Should you be up?"

"No," Tim said, cradling the arm that was attached to his injured shoulder, "but if I don't move too fast and I can stay out of Terry's way I'll be all right."

Tim walked closer to them and stopped in front of Clint.

"I don't blame you for going into town, Clint. If you're not a logger, this kind of life can drive you crazy."

"I'll be back," Clint promised.

"Maybe, maybe not," Tim said.

"What do you mean?" Tod asked.

Tim said, "I think our friend here has another motive in mind for going into town."

"What?" Tod asked, while Clint seemed to ignore both of them.

"I think he wants to push Ransom into making a move, and he can't do that from up here."

"Is that true?" Tod asked.

Clint turned and said, "Tim sounds a little feverish to me, Tod. You'd better get him back to bed."

"You've killed for us already, Clint," Tim said. "We never wanted that, and we want you to get killed even less. Why don't you just keep riding right on through town and leave?"

Clint shook his head and looked Tim in the eye.

"Tim, you've got a pretty exaggerated opinion of what I'll do for you," he said. "I can assure you that if I should kill Bennett Ransom, it won't be for you, it'll be because if I don't, he'd kill me. It's that simple."

"Sure, Clint," Tim Battles said. "Hell, that's so simple even a dumb logger like me can understand it."

"I hope you do," Clint said. He turned and climbed up on Duke's back. "I'll see you fellas soon."

As he rode off Terry came up on her brothers and asked anxiously, "Where's he going?"

"To town," Tod said.

"To do what?"

Tim Battles looked at his sister and said, "To do what he's been doing most of his life, I guess."

"What's that?" Tod asked.

"Kill, or be killed."

FORTY

While Clint Adams was leaving the Battles camp to go to Olympia, trouble rode into that town on a steel dust horse.

His name was Bill Wallmann. It was a simple name, and no one had ever found a nickname—like "Wild Bill" or "Kid" or "The Irish Gun"—for this man.

Unless it was "Death."

FORTY-ONE

Deacon Platt was in his usual place, watching for Clint Adams. When he saw the man on the steel dust ride in, he sat forward and said, "Shit," under his breath.

For a moment he was confused. He knew Bill Wallmann when he saw him because he had seen him once before. You don't forget a man like that. His confusion lay in his indecision over who he should tell about this new development, Bennett Ransom or McCoy.

It was then that Deacon Platt had his first intelligent thought ever.

Why would a man like Bennett Ransom send for a man like Bill Wallmann? The answer? He wouldn't.

Platt stood up and, hoping that Wallmann would not spot him, sidled down the street towards the bank.

When Clint Adams rode into town, Wallmann was already in with the man who sent for him, and his steel dust was already in the livery. When Clint left Duke off there he spotted the other horse, and it seemed to strike a familiar chord in his memory. He couldn't pin it

down at that moment, so he shrugged and walked over
to the saloon where Candace worked.

"I'm glad you could make it so soon," McCoy said
to Wallmann.

"You said something about a lot of money,"
Wallmann said. He was sitting across from McCoy's
desk, and McCoy had made no mention of that fact.
Not with this man. The banker knew who he was
dealing with this time. He'd wired a friend of his for
whom Wallmann worked for and asked to "borrow"
the man.

McCoy knew that Bill Wallmann was like a lit stick
of dynamite, and he wanted to make use of him, pay
him, and get rid of him as soon as he could.

"A lot of money," McCoy said to the tall, thin
gunman, "and all you have to do for it is kill two
men."

"Killing's what I do best, Mr. McCoy," Wallmann
said.

"I know that, Wallmann," McCoy said. "Will you
answer a question for me?"

"You're paying for the privilege," the man replied.

"Do you enjoy it?"

"Killing?"

"Yes."

Wallmann made a face and said, "No."

"Why do you do it, then?"

"It's what I do best," Wallmann explained matter-
of-factly. "I'd be a fool not to make my living doing
what I do best."

That McCoy could deal with, unlike the perversity
of Bennett Ransom.

"Who do I have to kill?"

"A man named Bennett Ransom. Do you know him?"

"I've heard the name," Wallmann said. "Fancies himself handy with a gun."

"Can you take him?"

Wallmann's mouth moved, and McCoy thought that it must have been as close to a smile as the man ever got.

"They's only two men in the world I'd be a fool to draw on, Mr. McCoy. One of them is dead, and Ransom ain't the other one."

"Who's the dead one?"

"Hickok."

"And the other?"

"That ain't important," Wallmann said, and his tone clearly implied that he'd rather not discuss it further. "Who's the other man you want me to kill?"

"You'll have to get past Ransom first," McCoy told him.

"We're past Ransom, Mr. McCoy," Wallmann said, "and we're up to the next man. What's his name?"

"Clint Adams."

Wallmann's mouth moved again.

"They call him—"

"I know what they call him," Wallmann said, standing up. "When do you want Ransom killed?"

"As soon as possible."

"Then I'd better get to it. Where is he?"

"Probably at the saloon."

"There are two," Wallmann said. He'd noticed that while riding into town, just as he'd noticed the man creeping along the boardwalk towards the bank, trying not to be noticed. "Which one would he be in?"

"Cooper's," McCoy said. "He's at Cooper's."

"Cooper's," Wallmann said. "I'll take the money for the first one in advance."

"In advance?" McCoy asked.

"Yes."

McCoy's first instinct was to argue, but he quelled that and simply said, "I don't usually do this," as he took a stack of money out of his desk drawer and handed it to the other man.

"Well," Wallmann said, tucking the money away, "if I don't earn it you can take it off my body, can't you?"

As Wallmann left the office McCoy said—although the very thought disgusted him—"Yes, I suppose I could . . . if you don't get blood all over it."

FORTY-TWO

By the time Bill Wallmann left McCoy's office, Clint Adams was already in bed with Candace.

When he had entered the saloon she had said, "Well, have you come to pay me?" and that was all it took.

Candace was certainly knowledgeable in the many ways there were to get a man ready. She had Clint lie on his back and instructed him not to move unless it was absolutely necessary.

"I'm going to get you ready," she told him, and then went to work on him, using her hands, her mouth and, on occasion, even her feet.

"God, Candace," he moaned. She was cupping his testicles in one hand, and had a tight hold on the base of his cock with the other while she slid him in and out of her warm, eager mouth.

"Mmmm," she answered him, continuing to increase the suction she was exerting.

Everytime it seemed that he was beyond the point of no return, she exerted pressure on the base of his penis, and his urge to come abated. After she had done that for the third time, however, the pleasure of it started to mingle with the pain.

"All right," she said, finally, "I think you're ready."

"I'll say," he answered.

She climbed aboard him and, without preamble, guided his rigid column of flesh up into her. Coming down on him with all of her weight she drove him in as far as he could go.

"Yes," she said, throwing her head back, "oh yes, Clint, that's it."

"That's what?" he replied. "You're doing all the work, remember?"

"This is not work," she told him, increasing the tempo of her movements, "believe me."

"Can I move now?" he asked.

"You can do anything you want now, Clint," she said with her eyes closed. "Anything!"

"Good," he said, and with a buck of his hips he threw her off of him and flipped her over on her back.

"Hey!" she cried out.

"Don't worry," he said, climbing atop her, "now you're going to get paid."

"Good!"

She opened her legs for him and he entered her like a hot knife going through butter. In fact, that's what her cunt felt like it was lined with, hot butter.

"Oh, yes," she cried, "that's it, Clint, that's it. Pay me what you owe me."

He slid his hands beneath her to cup her firm cheeks and proceeded to pull her to him while he tried to go even deeper than was humanly possible.

"Oh, Jesus," she moaned aloud, "it feels like

you're splitting me apart.''

"I'll ease up, if you like," he told her, always considerate of his bed partner's pleasure.

"Hell no, man!" she replied. "Plow me to your heart's content, Clint. I've finally got you right where I want you."

"Oh really?" he asked. "And . . . where's . . . that?"

"Ohhh. I'll tell you . . . later . . . ohh God, yes!" she screamed, and suddenly she was doing the bucking, as if trying to throw him completely off the bed.

"Oh, God, I feel you coming," she cried out as he felt a torrent of semen rush from his penis to fill her up. "Oh, I can feel it!"

"Will you tell me now?" he asked, only moments after they had finished.

"Tell you what?" she asked.

"Just where it is you think you have me," he said. "You said you have me where you want me."

"Where I've wanted you ever since that first day," she said, "when you told me you don't pay for your pleasures."

"So?"

"So what do you think you just did?" she demanded. "You said yourself you were paying me—oh, not with money, I know, but you paid me!"

She was sitting up in bed now, staring down at him triumphantly.

What she expected from him he didn't know, but he simply sat there and admired the fullness and roundness of her impressive breasts, the pink nipples of which were still hard.

"Well?" she asked.

"Well what?"

"What do you have to say?" she asked, a look of exasperation taking over her lovely face.

"You're right," he finally said.

"Ah-hah!"

"I did pay you just now," he went on as if she hadn't cried out triumphantly, "but I paid you for a service—"

"Right!"

"—that had nothing to do with sex," he finished.

"What?"

He laughed and said, "I didn't pay you for sex, Candace, I paid you for doing a job for me."

"What?" she asked again, looking at him in disbelief.

"I didn't pay you money for sex, I paid you sex for a service," he said.

She stared at him in silence then, and he could see the truth dawning on her.

"Well, I'll be damned," she said, dropping down onto her back. "You are one sneaky bastard, Clint Adams."

"Thought you had me that time, huh?" Clint asked, feeling relaxed for the first time in weeks.

"I thought I did," she admitted, "but I guess I was wrong."

"I guess you were," he said, "and I'll tell you something else that just occurred to me."

"What's that?"

"I just used sex to pay you for a service," he said.

"So, you already said that," she replied. "Don't rub it in."

"Don't you see what that means?"

"What?"

He sat up and stared down at her and explained, "Candace, in this instance, that makes *me* the whore!"

FORTY-THREE

Bill Wallmann knew who Bennett Ransom was. He knew that Ransom had been called "the Baby-Faced Killer," as ridiculous a nickname as he had ever heard.

Wallmann was in his late thirties, a tall, slender man dressed in black, and when he entered Cooper's saloon he drew the attention of every man in the room—including Bennett Ransom, who was seated at a corner table with Deacon Platt and Joe Earle.

"There he is," Platt said to the other two men with him. "What did I tell you?"

"He looks like a son of a bitch," Earle said.

"Shut up!" Ransom hissed. He was studying Wallmann, and didn't want his concentration broken.

Wallmann walked up to the bar and caught the bartender's eye, motioning for a drink.

"What'll you have?" Cooper asked.

"Whiskey."

"A bottle?"

"A glass," Wallmann said. "Just one drink."

Cooper served the killer his drink, trying to avoid looking into the man's eyes. Cooper had been around, and he had seen Wallmann in action once. He felt that neither Ransom nor the Gunsmith would stand a chance against Bill Wallmann, and the man had to be here for one of them.

Wallmann knocked back his whiskey, put the glass down and then looked at Cooper.

"Hey, old man."

"Yes, sir?" Cooper asked, looking at the man's forehead. "Can I get you another drink?"

"No," Wallmann said, "no drink. I'm looking for a man and I heard he might be in here."

"W-what's his name?"

"Ransom," Wallmann said. "Bennett Ransom."

"Uh—" Cooper said.

"Is he here?"

"Y-yes, sir," Cooper said. "Back table, sitting with two other men."

Wallmann dropped the money for the drink on the bar and said, "Thanks."

He turned around, spotted the rear table with three men seated at it and approached it.

"Which one of you is Ransom?" he asked.

"I'm Ransom," the smooth-faced man answered. That much Wallmann had guessed. "What can I do for you?"

"You can meet me outside, in the street."

Ransom grinned and said, "What for?"

"I'm gonna kill you."

The smile disappeared and Ransom said again, "What for?"

"Nothing personal," Wallmann said. "It's just a job."

"You're Wallmann, aren't you?" Ransom asked.

"That's right."

"You know my name, Wallmann," Ransom said,

"but do you know who I am?"

"A snot-nosed kid who thinks he's a hand with a gun," Wallmann replied emotionlessly.

Ransom's face reddened and he demanded, "What's the matter, Adams afraid to face me himself? He's got to hire you to do his killing for him?"

"I don't know what you're talking about, Ransom," Wallmann said. "A man named McCoy hired me to kill you, and I intend to do my job. Do you want it in here or outside?"

"McCoy?" Ransom said in disbelief. It only took a split second for him to realize that it wasn't really so unbelievable. McCoy was afraid of him, and was looking to break up their "partnership."

"All right, Wallmann," Ransom said. "I'll meet you outside as soon as I finish this beer."

"Fine." Wallmann turned his back on Ransom without fear and walked out of the saloon.

"You gonna meet him, Ransom?" Platt asked.

"I'm gonna kill him, Platt," Ransom said, "and then I'm gonna kill McCoy." He looked at the two men and said, "You two get lost now. I've got to concentrate."

Platt and Earle rose and left the saloon. Wallmann was standing in the middle of the street, and they crossed over and took up positions where they would be able to see everything.

"What happens to our bet if Wallmann kills Ransom?" Earle asked.

Platt shrugged.

"I'll take Ransom against Wallmann, if you want," Platt said. "If he wins, our bet on him against Adams is still on."

Earle thought a moment, then said, "All right, I

haven't seen Wallmann in action, but I've heard of him. You're on.''

While Wallmann was waiting in the street for Ransom, Terry Battles rode into town, with the intention of keeping Clint Adams from getting killed. When she saw the man in black standing in the street, her heart sank. She didn't know who he was, but she had the feeling that something was happening, and she was too late to stop it.

Clint Adams was buttoning his shirt as he walked to the window of Candace's room and looked down onto the street. When he saw the dark-clad man, he knew why the steel dust in the livery had touched off something familiar in his head.

''Wallmann,'' he said.

He thought that perhaps the man was waiting in the street for him, but just then Bennett Ransom exited the saloon and nodded at Wallmann, who nodded back.

''What the hell—?'' Clint said.

''What is it?'' Candace asked from the bed.

''I don't know,'' Clint said, grabbing his gunbelt, ''but I aim to find out.''

By the time he made it down to the street the two men were beyond the point of being stopped, and he could only watch and wait.

Ransom's feet weren't planted a second when Wallmann's right hand sped for his gun.

Bennett Ransom went for his own gun, but he knew he would be too late.

He knew he was a dead man.

● ● ●

The onlookers were stunned as Bennett Ransom crumpled to the ground, his gun still in his holster. It was not death that had stunned them, but the speed with which it had come.

"Jesus," Deacon Platt said.

"I never seen anything so fast," Joe Earle said.

Platt swallowed. He had seen Wallmann before, once, but the man was even faster than he had remembered. It was inhuman for anyone to be that fast.

"I, uh, guess I owe you money," Platt said.

That was when they both spotted the Gunsmith standing across the street.

"I'll take Adams," Platt said then. "Double or nothing."

"Against that move?" Earle asked, looking at his friend as if he was crazy.

Platt looked at Earle and said, "I'm a gambler, Joe. Double or nothing, what do you say?"

Earle shrugged and said, "I still don't believe what I just saw. Ransom was damned fast, and he never cleared leather."

"What do you say?"

"You're on, Deke," Earle said. "You're on."

Clint Adams had kept his eyes on Bill Wallmann the whole time, because he was certain Wallmann would win. He had heard of Wallmann, heard his name mentioned in the same breath with Wild Bill, Warren Murphy and himself, but this was the first time he had ever seen the man in action.

Now he knew how Wallmann had gotten his reputation.

Wallmann holstered his gun, then turned his head just enough so that he could look at Clint Adams. The

Gunsmith met the other man's gaze and held it and although it was Wallmann who broke the contact, Clint was sure it wasn't because of any lack of confidence, or indecision on his part.

He watched as Wallmann turned and started in the direction of the bank. McCoy had watched the entire proceedings from in front of that building, and now had a look of great satisfaction on his face. He turned and went inside the bank, and after a few moments Wallmann followed him in.

Clint Adams was unaware that Terry Battles had spotted him from across the street and was coming over, or that Candace had come out the door behind him. He was remembering something he had heard about Bill Wallmann.

The man always got paid in advance.

FORTY-FOUR

"Clint, you've got to leave now," Terry said, tugging on his right arm. Before he realized it, he had yanked his arm away from her, causing her to back up a step.

"Don't worry, sweetie," Candace said. "He just doesn't want you hanging on his gun arm."

Terry looked at Candace, and then back at Clint, with fear plain in her eyes.

"You've got to leave," she said again. "We won't blame you."

"I can't," he said.

"He'll kill you," Terry insisted, "just like he killed Ransom."

"Maybe," Clint said, "but I still can't leave. Especially not now."

"Why not?"

"He's got a reputation," Candace said, "and so has the other guy."

"You recognized him?" Clint asked.

"I've worked around, Clint," she said. "I haven't always been in this town. I haven't seen him before, but I know who he is."

"Who is he?" Terry asked.

"His name's Wallmann," Candace answered.

Terry shook her head impatiently and said, "I don't know who he is, but I know he's dangerous. He went into McCoy's bank, that means when he comes out he's going to be looking for you."

"Maybe," he said again, and it was maddening to Terry that he could say that one word so calmly.

"I don't understand—" she started to say, but Candace broke in before she could finish.

"None of us do, honey," Candace said. "Only they do. Only Wallmann, the Gunsmith, Wild Bill Hickok—only they understand the things that men like them have to do."

"You're wrong," Clint said then, looking at Candace. "You're wrong. We don't always understand the things we have to do, but we do them anyway."

"You can't do this," McCoy shouted at Bill Wallmann. He jumped up from his seat behind his desk and said, "You've killed Ransom, I don't have anyone else."

"Mister," Wallmann said, "I'd be a fool to do anything else. The odds aren't good."

"But you're fast," McCoy argued, "I saw you. You're incredibly fast."

"I'm alive for two reasons," Wallmann said. "I'm fast, and I'm not stupid. What you're asking me to do is stupid."

"But if you don't do it, how will I get anyone else to?" McCoy demanded. "Don't you realize you're costing me a mountain?"

"Mister," Wallmann said, "if you can't take that mountain, if you can't take what you want, it's because you don't want it bad enough.''

"I'll double your pay," McCoy said.

Wallmann decided that there wasn't any use in talking to the man any further, and turned to leave.

"I'll triple it!" McCoy shouted as Wallmann left his office.

Wallmann kept walking.

Clint and Terry both looked and saw Wallmann walking their way.

"It's too late," Terry said.

They were all surprised when Wallmann reached them, passed them, and kept on walking without casting a glance towards Clint.

"Where's he going?" Terry asked.

Clint didn't know, but he watched as Wallmann walked to the livery and went inside. He was inside for the length of time it took to saddle a horse, and then he rode out on his steel dust.

The Gunsmith watched as Wallmann rode down the street towards him, and pulled his horse to a stop directly in front of him. Unconsciously, both women moved away from Clint's side.

"Adams," Wallmann said, nodding.

"Wallmann."

"I don't know what the beef was you had with that banker," Wallmann said, "but I think it's just about over."

"Glad to hear it," Clint said.

"I'll be seeing you," Wallmann said.

The Gunsmith nodded and said, "I hope not."

Wallmann turned his horse back in the direction of the livery, preparing to ride out of town, but he was stopped by Terry Battles.

"Wait!" she called.

Wallmann looked at her and she shivered.

"Ma'am?"

"I don't understand," she said. "What happened? Why are you riding out without . . . without . . ."

Wallmann looked at Clint, who simply shrugged.

"Ma'am, I'll tell you what I told the banker, just so you'll be able to sleep easier," Wallmann said. "In my whole life I've only known of two men I'd be a fool to draw against. You see, there's always someone faster than you, no matter how fast you are, and it's just plain stupidity to chance drawing against them. In my case, they's only two possibilities. Bill Hickok was one, and he's dead."

When he didn't speak further Terry said, "And the other?"

Wallmann looked at the Gunsmith again, and his mouth moved. Then he looked at Terry and Candace, touched his hand to his hat and said, "Good day, ladies."

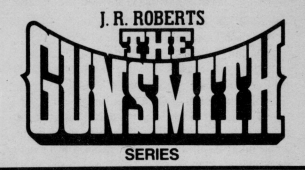

J. R. ROBERTS
THE GUNSMITH
SERIES

Prices may be slightly higher in Canada.